Praise for *Springer's Progress*

"High style and literary madness . . . Amoral and groiny as the subject may be, the real morality is in the writing, so strict, so caring, so classically grounded and conversant, so redemptive of the threatened sources of literature . . . rare, singular, deluxe." —Seymour Krim

"Immensely endearing . . . And how nice to hear two people actually laugh during sex."—*Ms.*

"Marvelously bawdy . . . but what stands out finally is the finely honed prose of a writer with a rare wit."—*Library Journal*

"As amoral and exuberant as if it were told by Dylan Thomas to the Wife of Bath . . . fills one with as much awe as laughter." —Douglas Day

"So rich in allusions, precision puns, extraordinary metaphors, Joycean wordplay, yeasty quotes and breathtaking prose and poetry that a lesser writer than David Markson would merely dazzle the reader."—Les Whitten

Also by David Markson

NOVELS

The Ballad of Dingus Magee
Going Down
Reader's Block
Wittgenstein's Mistress

CRITICISM

Malcolm Lowry's Volcano: Myth, Symbol, Meaning

ENTERTAINMENTS

Epitaph for a Tramp
Epitaph for a Dead Beat
Miss Doll, Go Home

POETRY

Collected Poems

Springer's Progress

David Markson

Dalkey Archive Press

First published by Holt, Rinehart and Winston, 1977
Copyright © 1977, 1990 by David Markson
First paperback edition, 1990
Second edition, 1999

Library of Congress Cataloging-in-Publication Data:

Markson, David.
    Springer's progress / by David Markson
    I. Title.
PS3563.A67S67   1990   813'.54—dc20   90-2731
ISBN: 1-56478-218-2

Partially funded by grants from the National Endowment for the Arts, a federal agency, and the Illinois Arts Council, a state agency.

NATIONAL
ENDOWMENT
FOR THE ARTS

Dalkey Archive Press
Illinois State University
Campus Box 4241
Normal, IL 61790-4241

Visit our website: www.dalkeyarchive.com

Printed on permanent/durable acid-free paper and bound in the United States of America.

Elaine.   How not?

That Sophocles was old when Archippe lived with him is proved by what her former lover Smicrines wittily said when asked what Archippe was doing: "As the owls sit upon the tombs so sits she."

—ATHENAEUS

Part One

There's Springer, sauntering through the wilderness of this world.

Lurking anent the maidens' shittery, more the truth of it. Eye out for this wench who's just ducked inside, this clodhopper Jessica Cornford.

Girl's a horse, stomps instead of walking. Most sedulously ill-dressed creature's ever wandered into the place also. Remorseless. Blouse tonight's all archaic frill, remnant from a misadvised Winslow Homer.

Paradox there, however. Catch her in repose and that profile's patrician. Unendurable cheekbones. When she's not lurching after that cow.

Tall, she is, and Springer's particularly enamored of her neck as well. Springer's a writer. Neck's sensuously *cartilaginous*.

Springer also sanguine about good boobs?

Dotes on such speculations, Springer does. Pretty much an intrinsic inflection of the saloon anyway. Joint's awash in authors, prime theme indisputably'd be *gelt*. Pussy and/or baseball running a tight second, however.

And after all Springer's forty-seven.

Then again, actually gets his share. Man's handsome as coin. Portrait of him decomposing in an attic somewhere, even been hinted.

No planner, though, and whatever he falls into's what he'll fall into. Renders Cornford a unique proposition, since they've been kicking something around for months now, and professedly on the up and up. Girl's a remarkably accomplished editor for her years, on the staff of a political weekly Springer never reads. But now she's also into her first novel and wants to talk.

Admires Springer's last, she's said. Decided aura of wit

about her for that alone, only nine or thirteen of the century's other readers in accord. Calamity.

Source of such manifold depressions as beset him these days too, most like. Hundred sketchy pages of another in his desk, hasn't riffled the manuscript since summer. When'd it get to be February?

Angst's even turning palpable of late. Wife's working, Springer'll catch himself suppressing a neurotic giggle when he scrawls a check to cash and slinks over this way.

Rarely been known to deter him, however, saloon's his sanctuary. Hunting grounds as noted also, though Dana's scarcely to be informed of this last. Prototypic loutish male enclave, how she's mercifully dismissed it.

Not that Springer hasn't at least alluded to the question. His own sneaky guilt's what nudges him, or's he maybe fishing? Dane into any hanky-panky on the side herself?

Dana's an agent, latched in with steamy young Byronic mooncalves all hours of the month. Rubenesque's his kindly hyperbole for what her middle's become, and Springer'll now and then wistfully recall when her thighs were fabulous. Still, dresses shrewdly, face's striking. What he informs her's that no reasonably vesicular adult male can sustain an ostensible friendship with a woman and not eventually grope for her drawers.

"Lucien, your head has been twisted about these things since I met you. I'd take it as an affront to my position."

Can't be denied he's dropped one shoe nonetheless. Irreducible truth's that Springer'll hie his randy *tuchas* to the very grave amid visions of fair women.

Cornford being the moment's, that bone structure alone sufficient to break his heart where there she finally emerges. So now watch him feign immaculate surprise.

"Jessie, hey. How goes it?"

"Lucien, hello. Are you waiting for the little girls' room?"

[4]

"What time does it arrive?"

Brightest azure eyes and tawny bourbon hair, all that lumbering's a canard up close. Laughter's silvery too. "Good grief, now."

"I suspect I stole it. But listen. You be inclined toward a brief but poignant affair with a married man?"

"Why did I think we'd been talking about a literary friendship?"

"Ah, well. Seriously, wasn't I supposed to look at some manuscript? Why don't we finally do that evening?"

"This actually isn't a bad week for me, in fact. How's Thursday?"

"After dinner all right?"

"Say nine?"

"Get you a drink meanwhile?"

"No, thanks." Girl'll indicate the rear room. "I'm with someone."

Generally is. Remotely familiar television news face last week, viewing's less than Springer's sorest addiction. Tonight's an obscurely angular fair-haired sort with glasses, professorial.

"See you then."

Stride uncompromising again as he'll watch her away, hips a menace. Likewise the blouse, ought to have been immolated about the week of her menarche's his ultimate judgment.

Solve it Thursday? Bar's crowding up, how many others in sight he's solved long since?

Hold relatively sober and chances are he'll pursue none of them newly, however. One fairly inflexible precept, no protracted affairs.

Consider Norma Miljus, fleshly thirtyish feminist just now rumping by. Dour though dear friend of Cornford's, in fact, and seemingly impregnable. Or until Springer'd strolled casually homeward with her once of an auspicious

[5]

eleven P.M., and until the phenomenal mirthfully glandular three hours thereafter. Occasional sly wink in passing's the sum since, though, both well contented in the isolated impulse.

Again, what but *liking women* the ineludible essence here, there a known remedy? Dana hurting truly either, so long as nothing turns sticky? Springer's Talmud in a nutshell.

Fresh pour into his vodka, meanwhile, and abruptly he's auguring gloom anew. Filch a stool beside Lippman Pike, decides, house's good gray versifier. Of an age, they are, though Pike's all shaggy, might be a mentor. Springer'll fathom they've survived midnight if Pike tells him good morning.

"Morning, Loosh."

Twelve-seventeen. "Morning, Lipp."

"That visage meant to be somber?"

"On purpose. Might convince someone to talk me out of the leap."

"Poor lad. Enlighten the sensitive poet?"

"What's news? When am I going to get around to finishing that scabrous book, is all."

Miscalculation there, Springer's too late to retract. Son of man, seek not for solace in the tavern of thy peers. Sensitive Pike's all glee.

"Ah. And just what book are you reading, Lucien?" he'll ask sweetly.

Dinner dispatched a day later, Dana's ensconced in the bedroom. Some assiduous cocklepicker's manuscript at hand, most evenings devoured thus. Whence all these writers? Elect Springer literary imperator in his malaise of the moment, disembowelment'd greet anyone ventured beyond a solitary rhymed couplet per annum.

"Anything doing this Thursday?"

"I have that screening invitation. You didn't want to see the picture."

"What time will you be home?"

"Lucien, they're old enough to stay by themselves." Mild sighing thereupon, but relatively unserious. "The entire ambiance of Greenwich Village would warp if you missed one night in that place."

There's this should be recorded here about Springer too, man retreats at rebuff. Queer sort of irrelevant cranial displacement occurs, idiosyncratic fragments of art history be what pop into his mind more often than not. Dana get authentically grieved at him, find himself pondering that Michelangelo wore his boots to bed.

Modestly adept in other tinsel scholarly realms also, though he's just deciding a certain frontal strategy's due here instead. "Come on, Dane. Even when I'm blocked like this, who else except a writer sits around without seeing a soul all day? Take away that saloon and I'd go bonkers."

Tale's twice told, Dana's unimpressed. New tack demanded next in either case, sound put-upon should he? "Anyhow Thursday is something else. That girl, Jessica Cornford. I think I mentioned, she's into a novel. I finally couldn't say no."

Wet fingertip at the top sheet, attention back there already. Springer'll let well enough lie.

"Just don't spend any money," voice says, following.

Happy families are all alike.

Springer's mornings can be sportive too, anxiety's his perennial awakening benison. Booze being a depressant much help? Amy and young Doak clattering off, Dana out well before nine likewise. First inference of the accidie ahead and here comes that neurotic titter again.

Tolerance's extraordinary, though, rarely a hangover. Veil like gauze behind his corneas through coffee and the day's inaugural vodka, maybe. Amid catatonic ablutions he'll shit, liquescently, at least three times.

Compulsive neatness around the apartment'll squander some more time for him. Mostly sit with his feet propped on the typewriter, however, neighborhood Christy Brown here. Last time he'd announced even an incipient inclination toward work Pike deposited a gaudy package for him, back of the bar. Feather duster and a tin of machine oil.

Financial situation's emollient too. Dana's been at it less than three years, most of her clients still winning considerably more praise than copper. Household's in hock to the tune of seventeen thousand. Tune's a dirge.

All he needs, today a dismal inadvertent gag's returned to shrive him also. Months ago, last time his mother visited. There went Dane off to commence her ten-hour day, there lay Springer cretinous on five hours' sleep. Pillows punched to his ears, but he's hearing nonetheless. "I can't imagine what these so-called liberated women like Dana are thinking of. How independent will they feel with no one to support them in their old age?"

Corot painted approximately two thousand pictures. Three thousand of these are in American collections.

Swaddled in disheveled inertia anew, so next he's just hatching an epiphany. Indentured to that saloon for half a dozen years or so, amount of cash he's pissed away's got to be almost exactly the amount he owes.

Still waking like this to reality daily, there possibly a refund?

Cornford one more night away, and he's in a bookstore on Eighth Street, browsing. Visceral ache, this'll induce. Pike's latest leering at him from a rack, new ones by twenty other incorrigibles he's acquainted with also.

Jan Vermeer had eleven children. While near him two clerks eyeing someone, touch of awe. Then luxuriant lemon hair ahead he'd spot in Afghanistan.

Sidling up there, six months is it? "Shoplifting's indictable, lady."

Not swift enough. "Asshole." Avocado eyes he'll always forget the hue of, Springer's being kissed.

"No smutty books uptown?"

"Errands, errands. I almost did call." Hand on his, enduring warmth here. "Spring. How are you?"

"On the wagon, forty minutes at least. Come buy me one."

Clerks screwing up their courage, however. Slim tomes at thrust, her photo's jacketed athwart. "Ms. Oldring? Excuse me, do you have a moment to sign your poems?"

Squeezing Springer's elbow, ironic wink before she'll strut. Young together, they'd been. Customer or three clandestinely attentive now too.

Springer'll let himself idle outward, wait watching through the glass. Innocently familiar theatricality in the pantomime, Maggie's laughing ocher head be tossed back.

"God, you do thrive on it."

"Just bet your sweet *tush*."

Gesture then, it's three blocks. "Dana's home. Stop down?"

Lips pursed, Mag's pausing. Recognizes that twinkle too, something impish coming.

"Will they revoke my canonization, do you think, if I happen to mention that Arnold's in Chicago?"

Grin from Springer. Interminable between chances for them, dictum *re* prolonged affairs hardly germane. West End Avenue, he's flagging a cab.

"Or shouldn't we, Spring? Have I maybe gotten to like Dana too well in the past few years?"

"Get in here." Springer's amused. "Dumbbell. Don't you think I like her a lot better than you do?"

Uneasy Springer's betwixt another man's sheets, fourth spouse he's cuckolding of wayward Mag's. Ear half cocked for the key in the lock, that farce's overdue.

Guardian demon'll never let it occur. Special compartment of his psyche Oldring's been lodged in for too long, what's lasted's rare and nobody else's.

College girl when they'd met, and Springer a worldly twenty-five'd disdained her. Morning later she'd brazened his doorbell, transparent fib about no hot water in her shower, and a minute after that she'd bounded dripping into his bed. Springer'd dumped her on the rug.

Told her he'd be damned if he'd take her to the movies and hold her hand. Won him his edge, and crocodile tears had followed. Springer's been watching the legends grow since, however.

"God, what a certifiable bastard you were. If you'd known what I went through, building up the courage."

"All that phony sniveling."

"Fell for it though, didn't you? How long did I make that morning stretch out to?"

Springer's a figure in those legends too, he's heard, one true love who'd ever spurned her. Knows she knows better. Shared some hungers and some dreams, anything more's Maggie's own romanticizing. Terminal case, fuels such fables unabashedly herself.

Making Springer sad here tonight though. They'll meet at parties, last time alone together's longer ago than he'd recalled. Fragility behind her posings always, but an untamed antic wingèd thing's, he's always thought of it as. Now there's gauntness in her thighs, pelvis upthrusting beneath him's all bone.

Still, old Oldring. Memory in his member almost, homing. Mag's got him scissors'd. Sweat's breaking, they're easy and slow.

"Oh, Spring. Oh, Spring!"

Mouth's contorted, canary hair's wide flung. Springer's braced and sinewed as she comes and comes.

He too then, he'll burst into all that shuddering. Mag's wailed and locked him in, they'll collapse sunken and gasping.

"Oh, wow. Oh, thanks."

"The same."

"I mean it. Indubitably, like they say."

"Like who says?"

"Bad-penny Spring. I miss you now and again, do you know?"

Still panting into wisps at her neck, artery pulse there's slowing. He's begun to laugh softly.

"Always. What are you going to mock me about this time, *shmuck*?"

"Miss me like that summer, do you mean?"

"Which?"

"Whichever. When we split once and got together again. That dungeon you had on Waverly Place."

"I still don't follow?"

"Lying, Oldring. Bucket of fake tears then too. When you told me you'd had that abortion. 'Oh, Lucien, I was so horrendously alone!' "

"Oh, you skunk."

Clobbered by guilt, Springer'd been. Hour, at least, before he remembered a story she'd written, same spurious tactic for the heroine precisely.

Laughing herself now, navel's aquiver at his. Back then she'd flung things at him.

"I'm cursed. All the choice contaminating habits in this life, and what do I get but Springer?"

"You'll be eighty. We'll do piggy things on visiting day in the old ladies' home."

"I'm ready to believe it. It's funny though, you know?"

"What?"

"Time. Us. The way so little changes. Listen, tell me truthfully. Am I getting that way? Antique, sort of?"

"Dissonant Jesus." Question's canceled his membership, Springer'll roll aside for his drink.

"Do, Spring. Nobody else will be honest."

"I said it two decades ago. Your cheeks have a tendency to look puffy when you're on the sauce. Your mouth's crooked."

Contemplating lax flesh of a raised upper arm she's sitting now, she'll cradle a breast next. Doing so. "They sag, don't they?"

"Like Whistler's mother's." Vivid youthful Cézanne charcoal, in fact, he's reminded of. "Come on, Mag. Sexiest lady poet extant, didn't I read that somewhere? What they're calling literary criticism, these days."

"Up yours, friend."

"Limpid yet impenitent eyes. I swear I read that too. Johnsonian."

Gaiety abounding when she strikes at him, and Springer's snatching that wrist to jerk her down. "Fucker, you're jealous." Squirming beneath, Loosh won't relent until she's pinned. Then he's leaning in laughter to buss her lemony crotch.

On their elbows after that, fireside's all's missing where they'll nestle shoulder to shoulder. Other Oldring legends'd have her reamed by garrisons, why'd she never have a child? Springer devolving into wistfulness here, or's it just what's now in Maggie's face?

"You're right, I guess. You generally are. I'm a mess."

"Mildew on her soul. Now Oldring'll tell us how summer sang in her a little while, that in her sings no more."

"Edna St. Vincent Twaddle. True, though. I begin to half believe that *dreck* they peddle about me. Settling for devalued effects in my life and in my work both."

"Your work's okay. I notice you get it done."

Eyeing him at that. Mag'll turn avuncular at its implications, Springer's just missed a glorious opportunity to keep his mouth shut.

"Shit. That mean you're still not doing anything?"

Play deaf then. He remember the name of the man who broke Michelangelo's nose?

"God, it's sad."

Torrigiano. Fame's fame.

"I mean it, Spring. Your last one was so impossibly fine. Just because a couple of costermonger reviewers got lost in the maze."

"All right, Mag."

"What is it, then?"

"Existential decision. I'm experimenting in a new genre. Empty pages."

"Oh, crap. I'll tell you what half of it is, you're rotting. I'll bet this is the first time you've even been above the Village in months."

"I get the bends."

"Hurrah. Make it a game."

"Maggie, what do you want from me? I just can't work, is all."

"How does Dana feel?"

"She's used to it."

"Isn't she depressed?"

"She's busy."

"She's far too good for you, I hope you realize that? You still drinking as much as ever?"

"Look who's asking."

Taking a cigarette, eyes genuinely troubled. Springer guesses he knows she cares. Also knows Delacroix watched the feeding at the Paris zoo every afternoon, hobby maybe be some help?

"It's still so damned sad."

"World's out there waiting. Lost hieroglyphics of Springer the Babylonian. Everybody be redeemed."

"It's *you* it's important for, you ass. Oh, the devil with it." Up and collecting their glasses, she'll glower him a sigh. "I really do quit on you for an unregenerate bloody fool, sometimes."

Spring'll decide to accept that stolidly, even suspect he should have tried more poetry himself. No small degree of quaint truth you can compress into one line, looks as if.

Back with new drinks she's contrite. "Hell, Spring, ignore all that. You must feel disenfranchised enough without any dumb lecture from me."

Ungenerous extra lamp she's left on: does sag, this Mag. Striations at her hips, flirting with varicosity down below. Snows of yesteryear, Springer slouching deeper into melancholy yet?

"Maggie, I can't even read, anymore. Give me an hour, I might remember the last book that excited me."

"My gosh, you used to be insatiable. Four o'clock in the morning, I'll find some lunatic reference in my head, you're still the one I think about calling to ask."

"Ain't now as it hath been of yore, alas." Springer's laced his hands behind his neck. All the keen thirstings indeed, where and when'd he not notice the wells run dry?

"You know what I wish?" Perched at bed's edge Mag's pensive, child's kind of dreamy abstraction in the tracing of a knuckle at his groin. "I'd like to see you, once. I mean differently from a few tawdry illicit hours like this. Go away somewhere, say, just for a while. Shouldn't people have that, after so long?"

Languid, Springer's not answering. Fantasy's her province still, Mag's the sort believes she'll never die.

"You don't feel that way about me at all, though, do you? Spring? You didn't ever, really, did you?"

"Never had time. You were always such a slob I had to keep moving out."

Reinstituting laughter therewith, at least. "Oh, yes. Until you'd wind up without a pot, and I'd be the only one doltish enough to take you back."

"I'd have to wade through every soiled brassiere you'd discarded in months. You'd wake up to your period and

[18]

the only other sheets would be stuffed into the closet from the last one."

"Oh, you lie!"

"Happened."

"Wasn't I something then, though? I mean those early poems. God, I could write three sestinas waiting on line at the delicatessen. Wouldn't it have been gorgeous if I'd gotten consumption, say?"

"Prodigious. Who'd have noticed?"

"You would have, you cluck. Oh, how beautiful! Scarred forever, and I'd be your lost Lenore. Make you *feel* something, for a change."

"Maggie, I'm nine years older than Leopold Bloom. Try not to be crushed, but I've even got hemorrhoids. You want to skip the rest of this until after I shower?"

"Oh, Jesus, what a charade. Half a lifetime, my pearls before swine." Oldring's padding after him blithely, however, she's scooping up towels. "At least scrub my back then, swine. I ought to get that much out of you, after all these years."

Let Springer's skull wind up more out of joint than's ordinary, all sorts of quirky, disjunct quotations'll commence berthing in there, too. Take right now. Avoid running at all times, Leroy (Satchel) Paige.

England expects every man will do his duty. *Ibid.?*

Dodging another morning's redoubtable morning miseries, all he's up to. Helpmeet's hovering, however, familiar bedside catechism'll be inescapable.

"How late did you get in last night?"

"Dana, is there some reason I'm expected to make a note of it?"

Interrogation's devoid of any crass wifely suspicion, Springer's fairly certain, gist of it's weary reflex. Profligacy beside the point, anybody propose Dana ought to burst into hosannas over his sloth either?

Still, spiteful hundred watts twenty inches from his maggoty eyes, wretch truly need every lamp in the room?

Squinty three-quarter rear profile's what he's glomming her in, Springer considering fleshfolds she'll sheathe into disguise. Body-stocking'd.

Got the guilts today also, of course. Such as ever, immunized by exposure the patient'll survive. Creep crepuscularly on in pursuit of his own gamy ends, in fact, what he's about to do here.

"I told you I'd be out before you get back from that screening tonight?"

"There are frozen dinners."

This instance, what's fretting him's time. Case like Mag's, home by two-thirty or so, far's Dana's concerned he's been flanged to the floor at that saloon all night. How late's prudent if she's aware he's meeting Cornford to start with?

"I don't have much idea what the girl expects to talk

about, really. I'll probably head on over for a few drinks, afterwards."

Mumble's all he's vouchsafed, exotic Levantine tent seemingly being wriggled into now. Contingencies would appear fundamentally covered, however, Springer's the last of the Medici schemers.

"Aren't you getting up?"

"Honey, I'm wide awake."

Transformation's concluded meanwhile, tent's a pale cerulean caftan, in fact. Wily wench, looking regally slender, even. Blue's registering her corn-tinted hair all fleecy in contrast also, how's she devise those effects on no extravagance?

Cape and briefcase, blowing him a kiss. "I'm late. Call me?"

"This afternoon."

Truth be told, exemplarily handsome woman this ne'er-do-well's logged eighteen years with. Happen into his pub one witching hour, be after her ass in a trice himself.

Gather ye rosebuds while ye may. Martin Luther?

This be Springer? Block from Cornford's and his duo-
denum presuming coyness? Twitchy? Not possible.

Possible.

Thing's this. Halter some rutting mare in that saloon,
conclusion's mutually foregone. When's Springer actually
come courting last, however?

Reassuring local turf, at least, building he's passed a
hundred times. Up a superannuated elevator, investigate
a grubby dim corridor. *4B. J. Cornford.*

So who's this with the whorish pink curling device on
the top of her head, then?

"Hi, there. Come in. I was later than I thought. I'm
just finishing some dinner."

Already gathered, unless she's sucking those fingers
congenitally. Boiled workshirt's a triumph too. Springer'll
manage not to trip over the skis.

Kitchen's where he's led, and anal Loosh'll confront it
instantly askance. Wreck of the Hesperus. Bags, boxes,
cartons, crates. Need a manifest, where's provender end
and refuse begin?

Hamburger, she's been at. Mutilated tomato oozing glop
at center table, spillage of sugar beyond. Roaches unin-
timidated by mortal confluence.

"So. How've you been?"

Springer expected to stand here? Only other chair's
three grapefruit and a plate of anchovies.

"Oh, I'm fine. Let me just dump this." Coat's meant,
he'll venture elsewhere.

Balaclava greet him next, where'd she lug the six hundred
to? Debris a meter high on two overflowing file cabinets,
careless match be spectacular. Wounded couch against one

wall, ratty pillows scattered opposite. Books askew and adrift, phonograph records *aussi*. Abattoir.

Dinner dish being pyramided precariously atop others in the sink when he returns, thing's brimming. Springer's brought vodka. Did he? Summer solstice arrive before he locates it again.

"Oh, here." Succulently engaged with a greasy thumb this time, cracked cup's what he's tendered. "I hope you can do without ice? I forgot to fill the trays."

Garden of terrestrial delights, Springer's lucked into. Kettle's been on, girl's manufacturing instant coffee. Rip in her shirt, left underarm. Springer'll fix on that peep of flesh, elsewhere lies madness.

Puzzlement's his status, in part. Girl's best'd appear none too captivating, why's her diligent worst what she seems up to?

"Come inside, let's."

Let's. Home is where the flotsam is, two shakes and convivial Cornford's cozily crosslegged on the rug. Springer take an oath there's a rug? Random worn square footage attesting, bulk's periodicals and soda cans.

Girl's observing Springer observe, sigh of resignation's surely tired ritual. "Don't say it. Would you believe I have a woman who cleans every other week?"

"Must be a strain. I mean since her seeing-eye dog ran off."

Laughter's winningly unselfconscious, give her that. Glimmer of bare umbilicus mollifying his fastidious soul somewhat also? "John inside there?" he'll inquire.

"Oh, sure. Stinker. Go ahead."

Gander at the bedroom en route, in for any capital surprises? Bed not made, drawers jutting, raiment flung and heaped. Half emptied suitcase in the middle of the floor.

Half filled? Latrine be consistent too then, doubtless.

Doubtless. Tubes decapitated, jars unscrewed, month's towels and underwear molting. *Village Voice* shredded into squares atop the tank, though? Tricky stylish endeavor eluding him here?

Ah, well. Naturally. Virginia Woolf probably forget to dash out for toilet paper once in a while herself.

Springer's combing merely, he'll fake a flush. Forward, the Light Brigade. Weeks now, is it, girl's been a cynosure?

Then again. He truly able to fault her because his own metier's emptying ashtrays?

Scene shaping up anyway, mayhap? Disastrous curler abandoned now at least, there're those cheekbones. That neck also, Springer'd almost forgotten. Permissible to nurture a letch over the configuration of a larynx?

Foot they're off on, idle conversation'd almost seem a challenge, though. "So, Jessica Cornford?"

"So, Lucien Springer?"

Impelling gambit, now they can smirk at each other awhile.

Raincheck on it for the moment, fortunately, who's wedged between pillows on the couch but old Mag. Retrieve her as he sits.

"You into this?"

"Oldring? I'm an acolyte."

"What do you like?"

Thoughtfulness before she'll respond. "The way she really hurts when she's hurting, I guess. Irony, too. Like that story they're always anthologizing, do you know it?"

"Which?"

"This young girl, shacked up with someone who keeps bitching about what a mess the apartment is." Grin at that. "All right, personal identification. Still. When she finally decides to rip up the linoleum. Only it turns out like Ur of the Chaldees or someplace, a hundred layers."

Springer's laughing.

"What's funny? It's touching. The girl does try."

"I'm just remembering what Oldring left out."

"What do you mean?"

"When the poor simp she's living with is awarded the privilege of finishing the job. Days. And do you know what linoleum smells like when it's been rotting under there since Beowulf?"

Cornford's at her coffee, dawn on her slowly.

"Hey, you're kidding? You really went with her? When she was that young?"

"Jessie, it wasn't quite statutory."

"I never knew about that. Golly, what was she like, back then?"

"Fairly close to what's in those few stories, actually. Histrionic, sometimes. Though she'd quit when you saw through it. Fun. I like her."

Cornford's impressed. Cristoforo Springer discovering a new passage to the Indies here? Cable Maggie thanks, soon's he hails land.

"Was she as beautiful as she seems? Boy, the sensitivity in some of those early photos."

"Losing it a little. After all."

"That's sort of pleasing, you know?" Girl's unfolding upward. "I didn't think people did that, that long ago. Lived together, I mean."

"Now, *merde*."

"Sorry about that." Laughter'll trail, she's heading inside.

Tennis shoes left behind, Springer's noticed. Galumphing after that rambunctious cow still, however.

Vodka jug's what beckoned. "Nuts. I hate it without ice myself."

"Tell me what your novel is about."   •

"Sometimes I wish someone would tell me."

Opposite end of the couch this time, ankles being sat upon. Odd look of stringy dishevelment now also, or's chiaroscuro doing that? Lamp's back of her, girl's Italian movie-ish suddenly.

"Whose great line did I read? That he'd lost track of his intentions completely, though one of his intentions undoubtedly had been ·. write a book."

"Pretty funny. But tell me anyway."

"I feel awkward. Honestly. I'd much rather hear what you're doing."

"I told you in the saloon once. Slough of Despond."

"Damn it, Lucien, that's criminal. What *was* it about?"

"You. In ten or twelve years, say."

"I'm twenty-five. Do I turn out rich and adored?"

"Quick story. Woman I know, good-looking, maybe thirty-eight. Two divorces. One night she wasn't going to let me come over. She'd torn the apartment apart. Literally. Including the book that was all she had to get herself through the weekend with."

Cornford's attentive, casually rife with ulterior motives Springer'll continue. "Oh, I took her to bed, of course. We do, it works. Still, she knew I had to get out of there by two or three o'clock."

"Meaning she'd be right back where she started?"

"Worse, maybe. Who knows?"

"And that's it?"

"Was it. Corner somebody near the breaking point like that, was all. Try and manipulate that stress."

"Be tough." Mirth's back abruptly. "Thanks. I can't wait."

"Tell me your life story and I'll change the whole thing. Inspire me."

"Such as how?"

"Seriously. Why you're not at least living with someone yourself?"

"Oh, well, who hasn't? In fact I'm going away with one of them for a few days tomorrow."

Barrier there? Springer'll wait while she replenishes vodka, girl's a gulper.

"One of those things that never quite came off. But there's a lot of residual affection."

"Nobody else urgent?"

[27]

"Urgent, no. I do see several people, though."

"You still haven't said what the novel's about."

"God, you're persistent. Just the usual pale and wan former virgin, I'm afraid. Pretty, sort of crazy. Trying to figure out why she's so screwed up. Shit, how do you reduce it that way without sounding retarded? I'm also incidentally learning that I can't plot my way into the bathroom and back."

"You want me to look through some of it?"

"Lucien, would you? I'd really be grateful." Wry glance at those dehiscent file cabinets. "If I can even find it all."

"Some other time. What happens if I'm not rhapsodic about what I read?"

"Have some apostolic friend request a requiem. Go limping tearfully on, however, if that's what you mean?"

Springer beginning to like her? Some while since's the fact of it. Drawn to that despoiled look too, hard put to pin it down. Oldring's a Botticelli for him, Dana's all old Delft sunlight through a casement. Eyes too blue here, contradiction. Aristocratic Gauguin make any sense?

"I'm just thinking. Would you like to meet Maggie, for any reason?"

"I don't know. Should I? People usually break wind, or something. Do you still see her often?"

"Not that much. By chance just last night, though. It's good, a lot's lasted."

Considering that, expression's peculiarly pursed.

"I sense an insinuation over there, woman?"

"You tell me. All these *good* relationships that keep getting mentioned."

"And?"

Cheshire cat then, all twinkle. "Why, I'd be enchanted to chat with you about my writing, young lady. So long as I can make a few other raunchy proclivities clear in passing."

[28]

"Oh, Christ. Wait for me at the next corner, will you?"

Both laughing. "So? Finish it. Did you, then?"

"Did I what?"

"Screw Maggie Oldring last night?"

"You're the smart ass. Solve it yourself."

"Never mind. I might just dig out that manuscript and make you read it now after all."

"Too late. Get over here."

Coming. All amused congruity where she's swinging about, shoulder'll be at his hip.

"Sophisticated novelist. Man's an open book."

"About to take you to bed, though. I look distressed?"

Kissing the girl's laughter then, Springer'll slip inside that shirt. Heft there, surprising. Mouth's voluptuously incontinent, not.

"Good God."

"Lucien, what?"

"What did you do to that hamburger? You *reek* of garlic."

"Oh, heavens. Be my guest." Cornford's shaking with delight. *"Honi soit qui* smell *y pense,* can I say?"

Clasping him down at that, merrily omnivorous she'll devour him. Springer's but to do or die where they're slobbering and slobbering.

Hunch, he's getting. May survive.

Other side of the looking-glass is where Springer's gotten to next, matter of fact. Color him slackjawed.

Where Cornford's gotten's out of her skivvies. Girl's possessed of the most unimaginably beautiful body he's seen in his caterwauling life.

Fact. *Nolo contendere.*

"What, Lucien?"

Hands lifting to his cheeks, almost as tall as he and her eyes warmly gleamy in the diffuse bedroom light. That be a tardy smidgen of shyness in her smile too? Springer'll kiss her sweetly for it.

Still. Nonetheless. Be that as it may.

"Go away. Stand across the room. No, wait. Here. Lie down."

"Lucien, what are you talking about?"

Compliant, however. Rabbit hutch there, she's tossing aside blankets.

"Just lie there. On your back. Yes. Don't move."

"Oh, please. You're embarrassing me. I'm at least a dozen pounds overweight."

"Jessica, you are out of your bleeding mind."

Trust Springer, one territory where the man's a connoisseur. Composite he's even toyed with, anatomy recollected in tranquility. Bosom from an old lay here, hip there, convexity of a calf from elsewhere still. Cornford's just wiped out the lot of them.

"Lucien, I feel silly. I have jodhpur thighs, even."

"Just be still. I'm writing a poem. What's a rhyme for light under a bushel?"

"Oh, stop. Anyway, there isn't one."

"Has to be. How else do you perpetuate an aesthetic experience?"

Meaning that, astonishment's upon him yet. Longest lithe legs, Modigliani waist. Pelvic structure's what he's aching over, however. Girl's an archetype, all immemorial longings renewed right there.

"Lucien, do stop."

Philistines be his death. Circling to the bottom of the bed, suitcase'll almost send him sprawling also.

"Look where you're going at least, dodo."

Springer'll look where he will. Triangulation back to vaulted mystery's the leggy view from down here, crotch-on and the Delectable Hills beyond. Epochal, where're words?

"Beware the Jubjub bird, and shun the frumious Bandersnatch."

"Oh, you are insane. Will you come up here and kiss me?"

"I did that. You're smelly. Listen, would *sqooshal* be a rhyme?"

"Would what?"

"Ha. Sort of a sound and a smell both. Beats garlic any day. Wait."

Beamish boy there now, face-first into her vulva's where he's happily headed. Unwitting Cornford'll quiver and jerk, spasmy thighs'll crush his ears.

All's brillig thereafter though, Springer's amidst the slithy toves. All squishy and squirmy's his clitoral Cornford too.

Poet of the pudendum. Hark the sqooshal.

And what a liar's Loosh. Pox upon tidiness, true metier's this. Slurp and burble here till dawn.

So why's he beached and panting in moments instead? Medical profession looked into the effects of smoking on cunnilingus?

"Fucking cigarettes. Man's reach should exceed his gasp."

"Oh, Lord."

Vaginal slaver's all over his face where he's ascending. Slop it all over Cornford's, orifice to orifice in wanton wet initiation.

"The Jabberwock, with eyes of flame, came whiffling through the tulgey wood."

"I'm doomed. Do I really need this lunacy in my life?"

Adjusting while she's laughing, however, girl's getting them nested. How'd Springer slip inside there so fast? Sopping's why, elemental.

Further astonishment's in store still, though. "Holy smokes."

"What?"

"The way we fit."

Molded, they are. Grasp of their arms, even, Springer's finding it uncanny.

"I thought the same thing. It's only chance."

"Still. Fucking's fucking. This is *comfortable*."

Fucking's insidiously what they're already well about, however, lest Springer seriously not have noticed. Minute or two, proposition be earnest.

Is now. That sqooshal enterprise more efficacious than Springer'd known, girl's this swiftly almosting. Almosting? Squeeze the life out of him rather, oh tremendous, there they go bouncing down the bed.

Corrugated tin roof's what he means, Springer's hanging on for dear life next. Whole mattress's practically levitating.

"Oh, Lucien! *Oh, Lucien!*"

Sacrebleu, girl's a sensation. Crashing into a delirious broken moan at last, but exquisite contractions'll keep snatching at him even after. Lucien's ecstatic as a loon.

If Cornford's come, can Springer be far behind?

Just ask. Oh, wow. Oh, frabjous day.

"I owe a cock to Asclepius. You want to pay him for me, please?"

"I know what that is. Somebody's last words."

"Lucien Springer's. I just might take the hemlock myself."

"Apropos of what, may I ask?"

"Lack of perception. All the nights I've let you come traipsing into that saloon unmolested."

Laughing gently beneath him, breasts crushed and pillowy.

"Jessica Cornford."

"I presume."

"Answer me something. No. Don't."

"Some choice."

"Strangers, I see you with. Anybody I know?"

"People I've let molest me? Why?"

"Robinson Crusoe syndrome. Whose footprints on the sheets here?"

"Come on. The sheets I do remember to change. Most of the time. Anyway, you'll be surprised. There've only been nine or ten altogether. None you might know personally, I don't think. Should I ask you the same question?"

"Better not. I just remembered. Who's your closest friend over there?"

"Lucien, you didn't screw Norma Miljus?"

"Didn't I? What dire secret should I be informed of?"

"Oh, no, I love her. It's just that she's so intense. Didn't she quote Friedrich Engels or somebody all night?"

"Too many other oral pastimes intruding."

"Oh, how glorious. I think I'll tell her."

"Bless you."

"You know I wouldn't."

"Maybe I'll tell you something instead."

"Sounds ominous."

"The way you go stomping in and out. You're such a horse."

"Lucien, am I really?"

"Jericho. Walls come down. I think I'll tell you something else, too."

"You're certain you want to rush into it?"

"Whenas in silks my Jessica goes. You're generally somewhere between Mother Machree and Quasimodo."

"Oh, now wait, that I'll argue about. I'll admit I'm casual, yes. But who's not, these days?"

"No good. Even when you try a dress. Consolation prize at the Vladivostok harvest ball."

"Oh, good grief."

"Jessie, a ten-second glance in any direction. The next poor little match girl in the snow, even."

"Springer, how would you like to take a flying fuck?"

Eyes sparkling though, he's shifting slightly just above. Face's shadowed, renewal of that elusive ravagement in its contours also. Haunting, Springer's learning he can stare and stare.

"One other thing."

"I'm not listening."

"Do, Jess. You're so impossibly lovely at this instant I hurt from it."

Inhalation at that, she'll tighten where Springer's remained within. Springer'll lock against her in response.

"Good heavens. Lucien?"

"What, horse?"

"Can you again? This quickly, I mean?"

"Oh, Christ, do get back at me. About the year you were *born*, I could have."

Smoke's what they'll come unstuck for finally. Though Springer on hands and knees'll lick perspiration from her sternum while she's wriggling out from beneath.

"Mine are still out front, I think."

"Hallelujah. Jessie, wait."

"What?"

"Come back. I mean turn around."

"I thought we did this already?"

"Not this, we didn't. Just stand there now. Sainted Moses."

"Imbecile. Will you let me get cigarettes? A rear end is a rear end."

"Not this one. Stop squirming and let me explore."

"You *are* crazy, sort of."

"Jessica, I swear. It's so perfect it's incredible. Praxitelean. Lie down here again."

"Oh, Lordy. How now?"

"Obviously on your stomach, nitwit."

"I feel sillier than before."

"Shut up. Lift up, too."

"Like which?"

"Proctology. Just bend your knees. No, not your arms. Leave your head down."

"Lucien, where are you? Oh, no, you're not really?"

"Don't fight it. It's bigger than both of us. Besides which I can't stand it."

"God save me. You won't be able to. I thought you just said you couldn't this soon anyway?"

"Jessie, one unveiling of this and you could resurrect Archimedes. Listen, do you have anything? Vaseline, maybe?"

"Nothing. Unless. Oh, gleeps, I'm mad myself. Would margarine be any good?"

"*Quién sabe?* Never mind. Just lift up a little more, we'll make do with nature's own. Let me get back in where I was."

"Oh, my, resurrection is right. That's funny, didn't Archimedes have a lever, or something? *Ummm*, lovely."

"Fulcrum."

"Whatever. Nice man. But why don't we let's just do it this way, Lucien? Leave it where it is? Oh, stinker."

"Matter of fact Archimedes also had a screw. Made water run uphill. Stay the way you are, now. No. Spread some more."

"Lucien, it's not going to. I'm sure."

"Just relax. Unto the breach, dear friends. Jessie, hold still."

"Oh, dear."

"Once more. Or close the wall up with our English dead."

"Somebody. Help."

"You help. Just press backwards."

"Well, it hurts, sort of."

"Stiff upper lip."

"Stiff something else is the whole trouble."

"Half a league already. Onward. *Delenda est Carthago.*"

"I think I want my mother."

"Your mother do this?"

"You're dreadful."

"I'm also getting nowhere fast. Halfway's all."

"Isn't beauty only skin deep anyway?"

"Oh, *cojones*. Now it feels like if I push any more it'll break off."

"Soon, hopefully?"

"Cunt. It's fucking heartbreaking."

"You just said it was breaking something else."

"Hell. Move over. Let me lie down and cry."

"*Deo gratias.*"

"World's right. Failure. Art, life, now Jessica's sphincter."

"One part of you doesn't look very failed from this angle."

"Turn over again. I can at least just stare some more."

"I've got a better idea. Waste not, want not. *You* stay there, this time."

"Beware of Greeks bearing fulcrums. What are you doing? Come here."

"No. Stay on your back. Let me climb up."

"What he said was, give him a lever and a pulley and he could move the world. Here, wait. Let me."

"It's all right, I'm getting it. Oh, yes. *Oh*, yes. I think I'm skewered. Am I too heavy?"

"Anybody ever tell you about the old prostitute who sat down to rest on the fire hydrant? And sank slowly to the ground?"

"That's atrocious."

"Oh, man, Jessica the squatter. I can feel the very roof of you, up in there."

"It may well be my throat."

"Will it slip out if you sort of fold forward and let me hold you?"

"Ask Archimedes. Anyway, it wouldn't be the same. God, you can't imagine what it feels like so far in."

"Just keep writhing that way, I'll care less."

"We're awful. But don't you just love it?"

"I'm going to prove it in about twelve seconds. Six."

"Who isn't? Oh, Lucien!"

"Oh, Jessie!"

[*38*]

"Oh, yes! *Oh, yes!* Oh, hold me anyway, try to!"

Springer'll arch and heave to keep contained as she lurches. Does. In maniacal ricochet they're all grasped and wrestly then, they'll shudder and jounce and shiver and spurt.

Eureka! Out of the bathtub and into the street.

Truce. Battle fatigue. Damp head on Springer's shoulder, all's ebb and seepage.

Coition, attrition. "You really going away tomorrow?"

"Pennsylvania."

"How long?"

"Will it be five days? Yes."

"Hell. Tell me about him, a little."

"His name is Jonathan Hundley. I said, we lived together. In my last year at college. It's been a kind of intermittent habit, ever since."

"Ah, well. I suppose it can wait."

"What?"

"Second assault. Diabolical south slope of Mount Cornford. Can I advertise for Sherpa porters here in the Village?"

"You're impossible. Are you sure you're the same person who wrote those novels?"

"Priorities. This is important."

"Listen. Will you be brave if I tell you something?"

"Grace under pressure. Speak."

"I'm flattered. Truly. But I honestly suspect it just may not have been the most memorable experience in my life."

Subtler sort of ontological speculation next, however. Long-wedlocked Springer and that salubrious saloon, fuck and run's the wont. How's it happen he and Cornford are at it again?

Leavened this time as well, metronome where they're groined's *lentissimo.*

"I still can't get over it. How comfortable it is."

"You said that."

"I know. But three billion people out there, suppose everybody's matched? Go searching in Changchow, or someplace. And here's mine six blocks away on Bedford Street."

"It is strange. We're sort of *wrapped.*"

"Oh, hell."

"What?"

"Oh, nuts."

"Lucien, tell me?"

"Ah, Jessica. If you have tears, prepare to shed them now."

"Come on. Make sense."

"He was my friend, faithful and just to me. But Brutus says he was ambitious."

"Oh, glory. Are you sure? It doesn't feel that way?"

"Defunct."

"Aw, poor Lucien." Squirming and laughing she'll forage down there between.

Be salvaged? Not. Springer'll surrender and sigh.

"I'm obsolete. A third time's pure rumor."

"Everything was lovely. You're the noblest rumor of them all."

"I come to bury Caesar, not to praise him."

"Ambition should be made of sterner stuff."

"Oh, Christ. Enough."

"I apologize. But anyway. I could also tell you were concerned about *me*, not just screwing."

Girl right? Suspicion she may be. *Qué pasa aquí?*

"Ides of February. When do you leave tomorrow?"

"It's shameful. He's picking me up at seven in the morning. I haven't even finished packing."

"Really were supposed to get into Jamesian imagery, then?"

"I don't know. Were we?"

"Sorry?"

"You get dumber as the night goes on."

"When do you come home?"

"Tuesday night, sometime."

"Call you?"

"He might stay over, if it's late. He has to drive back to Boston."

"Jonathan the Intruder."

"Say hello to Lucien the Sodomite."

"Sodomy and justice for all. Listen, I'll get out of here. You're going to get about half a night's sleep as it is. There room for two in that shower?"

"I should really do the rest of my packing, first."

"May I?"

"I'd certainly hope so, dope."

Spray's commendable, Springer'll indulge himself. Culprit in him keep his hair dry, however. Freshly combed look be incriminating, chance Dana's awake.

Chuckle when he's toweled and emerging. Girl's sprawled over there and sleeping like a corpse. Considerate Springer'll make sure her alarm's set.

Hold up before he covers her, also. Cornford the clodhopper, joke's about four hours stale. Attic legend's in his mind now even, first drinking cup molded from Helen's breast. Recast it right here.

[42]

Still. *Veni, vici, veni.* Gaius Julius Springer, he'll head home from the Garlic Wars.

So why's he lingering?

About to tidy up and dust, is he?

Wide awake and time for a guiltless tinkle before Dana's departed now too? No esoteric evasions sprouting? What's with Loosh?

"So. How was your evening?"

"Oh, pleasant enough. She's a bright girl."

"Where did you go?"

"Some wet blanket warned me not to spend any money. We sat around at her place and talked."

"Did you, now? What's her novel like?"

"Sounded pretty commonplace, actually. I suppose I'll have to read it one of these days."

"Crafty. Give you a chance to see her again. You'll have a sweetheart."

Bequeath her a playful kiss at that, tip of the nose where she's waiting to exit. Solidest ground, he'll hop onto here.

"Oh, yes. Except she's just now going away for a while with some old boyfriend. A man she once lived with, in fact."

"Ah, well. Life treats you so unobligingly. I'll see you tonight."

Pause about to creep up on him thereafter, at least? Recall that Brutus was an honorable man, say? So are they all, all honorable men?

Hardly set him to skulking, however. Matter of fact he'll find himself feeling amazingly skittish instead, gift horse he'll decide not to look in the teeth. Come noon, jacket even be off the typewriter, all of two or three minutes.

No signature, envelope's chaste too. Simper when he strolls out to the box, but who's blocked-up Springer to contravene the muse?

Title's *On the Question of Jessica's Ass.*

Good Lord, thy bottom, lass,
That rump! The world
Goes round, I know, I know,
But asses, mostly, do not so.

Yes, asses, mostly, do not so,
For lasses, mostly, lump
Or sag. Canst make me fag
To love thy ass, thou being lass?

"Hello?"

"You're home. Did you get my poem?"

"Oh, hi. How are you? Yes, you dunce."

"I hope you understand it was one draft?"

"I hope so for your sake. Tell me what time it is?"

"Just after ten. I thought you might be at the magazine?"

"Oh, I've got an hour or so."

"Can I assume your boyfriend's gone?"

"Last night, yes."

"What are you doing tonight?"

"Well. I'm seeing a friend."

"I don't suppose you want to put it off?"

"I can't. Really. I already changed it once."

"I take it you mean a him?"

"Come on. I do know one or two."

"What about tomorrow?"

"What's today, Wednesday? Tomorrow's fine."

"Listen. I was going to bring you something. But I ought to know what brand."

"Lucien, you're broke, aren't you? Brand of what?"

"Toilet paper."

"Oh, go to the devil. And that's another thing, by the way."

"What is?"

"Galoot. It hurt all week."

Roguish countenance when she unlatches. Slobby old Cornford and that squirrel's-nest kitchen, Springer have the foggiest how delighted he'd be to be back here?

Nothing being voiced either, but what's this yeasty intrigue they're unquestionably in cahoots about? So sly and smickery when they kiss and confront? Seventeen seconds and Springer's up and under and unloading her brassiere, ne'er a blink at the onions, e'en.

"Good grief, will somebody look at us? Sublime to be exchanging ideas with you again, Professor Trilling."

"Just get your sublimity into bed."

"Lucien, wait. Among other things it's my period. Only this afternoon. I'm gushing."

"Among what other things?"

"Hmmm. Because it was just George Washington's birthday?"

"Stupe. Come on. Take the rest off."

"Oh, Lordy. How can anybody seem sophisticated one moment and not even housebroken the next?"

"When have I seemed sophisticated?"

"Let me think."

"Do it after you're out of those panties. There's an anthropology conference anxious for my monograph."

"About your mate from central China?"

"Wherever. Abyssinia. And on her dulcimer she played. Get down here."

"I guess I give in again. We do belong, somehow."

Packaged be a concept? Melded? Clavicle to fibula's the fit, transcendental.

"There such a word as transensualendental?"

"No. But now you might even like to say hello, would you?"

Springer'll windlass his puss out from nuzzling, they'll grin and grin.

"Hello, horse. Be informed. I missed you."

"My dulcimer, you missed. You're an inveterate horny old man."

"I am that. But it was queer. About six people in the saloon told me I looked perky or something during the week. Who are you?"

"Jessica Louise Cornford. I'm preserving it for the golden youth I'll wed."

"I'm *kvelling* for you. Listen. Tell me who you saw last night."

"Why should I?"

"Because I asked."

"Just a friend. His name is Max."

"Not sufficient."

"Nosy. He teaches philosphy. He's separated. He's sane."

"Sleep with him?"

"I just told you we're friends. Are you about to become some sort of nuisance?"

"You half said I could audit. Use it in my alleged novel."

"Do we make that work both ways?"

"Meaning?"

"Your wife. I hear about her sometimes, she's well thought of. Does she know where you are?"

"Not tonight. I did tell her last week, though."

"And?"

"*Nada.* You're writing a novel. You wanted to talk."

"How about otherwise. Does she know you cheat?"

"Jessie, I have no idea. She damned well should, after eighteen years. I guess she's simply convinced herself not. Did you mention your damaged aperture to your chum Jonathan, by the way?"

"You're changing the subject. At least give me a kiss and maybe I won't notice."

Mouths complemental also, gets almost creepy. Offer Springer world enough and time, savor all this for several millennia before he'll recollect to fornicate.

"Oniony bitch."

"Scallions, in fact. For remembrance."

"Sweet Ophelia. Anyhow, tell me about Pennsylvania too, what's his last name again?"

"Hundley. I've said, it's years. And no, I didn't tell him, lout."

"How often do you see him?"

"Oh, whenever. He lives with another woman, actually. We're like you and Maggie Oldring a little bit, maybe."

"But you're not in love with him?"

"He is with me, sort of. Lately he thinks he wants to marry me, even."

Springer's hiked himself onto his elbows, he's tracing fragile facial declivities with a knuckle.

"It's painful, but I'm outgrowing him in certain ways. He's an architect, and he's let himself become provincial."

"How about your sex life?"

"Good. Well, usually."

"This time?"

Cornford'll eye him, expression's ironical and resigned. "That's the usually part. He owns an old farmhouse over there. The only thing he had it in mind to do all week was screw. I can be disarmingly accommodating."

"But?"

"Who'd believe? All I kept doing was closing my eyes and seeing some specious married fuck-up named Springer."

20

How's Springer reacted to that? Girl serious? Just held her for all he's worth, howsoever.

"Jess, did you really?"

"It was being silly, is all."

"Never mind. You're beautiful."

End to that millennial browsing now too, he'll go clambering about for a handful of supple inner thigh. Divide and conquer. All moist and mossy where he's poking, trolls run off with the magical string?

"Lucien, you really shouldn't."

"Mind your own business."

"Whose would you say I'm minding?"

Slimy with uterine Jessica where he'll finally slither it loose, *de gustibus.* Springer's a peasant slave, erotic arousal at this ever.

"Foul deeds will rise."

"Oh, Lordy. Use one of those newspapers down there."

"Which? The one that says Vasco da Gama just got back?"

"Fink. Lucien, I really am a mess."

"Be your finest hour. Lie back."

"No. Wait, then. You."

Taking matters into her own hands, ah, yes, Springer'll grandly accede for the nonce. What's bottom-upward beside him but that inspirational seat of her charms as well, he's just commencing to fondle same when she's at him with her mouth.

Stately pleasure-dome decreed. Cat and mouse down there at first, tongue's flittery and will-o'-the-wisp. Ummm, emboldening, puckery small gulp or two now. Whereupon Springer's breath doth catch, girl's of a sudden beset to swallow him entire.

Saints preserve him, nearest of her limbs he'll snatch, he'll squeeze it to the bone.

Oh, indeedy, ye gads, all spittle and suck she's upon and upon, Springer's atingle to the soles of his feet. May just bite through his lower lip for the sheer nuance of it. Fervid for this, let him confess, heart's less where he eats than where he's eaten. Sappho, Cleopatra, Joan of Arc? Pre-eminent female ever lived's the Neolithic nymph first wondered would it taste nice.

Ah, dear gobbly Jess, just keep right on and he'll float into space. Xanadu's soon.

So why's he calling halt? Wanting Jessie's why, he'll rise and ease her around. Conjugating salivations in gratitude's part, mounting withal, he'll glide full fathom unhindered into the multitudinous seas incarnadine.

Madness in minutes then, how explain? How many thousand fucks in the days of Springer's years, what witchery's Cornford's alone?

"Oh, Jess! Oh, Jess!"

Springer's assassinated, headless corpse about to run amok if she allows. She won't, she won't. Leglocked and enswathed she's got him, he'll squander seed now until he's raving.

Alluvial Mesopotamia, eternal Euphrates, anyone about to heed? Springer's just invented agriculture.

Week ago was that? Entrails palpitating yet. This Cornford still soothing his watery spine from beneath?

"Oh, Lord. Too much, too much."

"Funny Lucien. Nice-funny, I mean. You almost make me feel as if I'm the first woman you've ever had."

"You may well have been. Oh, wow. Less good because you didn't, though."

"It doesn't matter. I knew I'd need a long time."

"I wish you had."

"I knew you did. That's why it doesn't matter."

"Charitable bullshitting Jessica."

"It's not. I told you. I was fucking all week. I'm all fucked out."

"Oh, Jesus, you are something."

"And those were mostly let's-pretend you, too."

They're laughing, Springer's kissing the this and that of her. Mastoid he'll dwell upon, nibble her ear. How fucking impossibly good he feels, no end.

"Jess, Jess, Jess."

"Lucien, Lucien, Lucien."

"Listen. I'm not even sure I've got the vaguest idea what this means. I'm also deranged. But can I say that I half think I'm in love with you?"

"Oh, Lucien, don't."

Tensing beneath him. He'll watch as her lips compress.

"You don't mean it anyway. Now we're both being silly."

"Oh, Christ. All right. I said I don't know what it means. But it was also *there*, damn it."

"Oh, dear."

Face's newly umbra'd, hint of that despoliation he's left unsolved. Or's it sadness now? Springer truly aware what he's flirting with, these moments? Who's Cornford? Only knows he's so contented here he aches.

"Would you get me a cigarette, please?"

"Of course."

Inguinal leakage about her loins, sheets like Caesar's mantle, she'll smile again in turn when he's indicating.

"Never mind me. Will you look at yourself?"

Assassinated for fair. Springer'll laugh and run a finger through, he'll taste menstrual Jessie on his tongue.

Honeydew.

21

He had several pupils, among them Andrea del Sarto, who counted for many. Line of Vasari's. On Piero di Cosimo.

Cody, Wyoming, Jackson Pollock was born in.

And what'll all this be about, pray tell?

Duration of the one smoke's all it's taken. Milk of Paradise, Springer's ass.

Younger Holbein had two children in London, wife and four more back in Basel. Where're Springer's?

Just gazing at her again's what's doing it also, flexure of a lifted calf's enough to spawn grief.

"Shit. What did I say? Transcendental sensuality?"

"Transensualendentalism, I think."

"Sort of sucks, as a sanction."

"I know, I guess."

"Do you?"

"It's begun showing. But you should be the one to say it, Lucien."

"Never happened before. Always so casual, like old Miljus, say. Or else I'm no more than into somebody's hose when I'm antsy about how soon I can split."

Hand'll falter against her hip, he'll fight the looking. Will he? "Oh, Jess, I don't want to leave here at all!"

Clutching her again then, Springer's miracle. Embrace this girl and he's come home from somewhere far.

"Damn it, damn it, damn it. I'd better. Right now."

Springer's so hung up his throat's tight. Impossible. Go.

"I have to. Oh, Christ."

No words? To voice what? Face's cast aside.

Not stirring when he'll withdraw either, break his heart. Swiftly, though, must, watch Jessie's blood race amid rivulets and evanesce at the drain. Sketching geometric perplexities with a stick in sand, old Archimedes, when a centurion speared him down. First towel at hand.

Girl's turned away since, in bleakest silence Springer'll dress.

"Jess?"

Oh, dear Jesus now, she weeping softly over there?

Damned be Springer, two nights, a lark. And yet she too? What yearning chord can they have struck?

"Jess? Listen, please. I'm sorry. It's just fucked up completely now. Are you okay?"

"Yes." She'll look to him finally, wan smile be forced. "I said, we were both inane. I do understand."

Clodhopper Jessie, dear horse. Wetted cheeks so wrenching, all hollow anew. Stay and minister until small laughter's back, at least?

And then?

"I'll make sure the latch clicks."

"Thank you."

Man who abused the block of marble Michelangelo'd later redeem into the *David* was Agostino di Duccio. Alone and untended during a plague's how Andrea del Sarto died.

Night's a sudden abomination of icy rain when Springer's down, wind's evil, when'd these maledictions commence?

He got some notion he deserves better, the prick?

Part Two

See homey Dana, panties only, some homily or other for the kids while she's hammocking herself into a brassiere. See the Hogarthian domestic niceties Springer'll arise to.

This a cold now also? Celestial. Best of all possible worlds.

"Oh, you're awake. I was going to call the butcher from the office. Will you pick it up before five or so?"

"Hell."

"Lucien, what else will you be doing?"

Cutting his throat in the church. "Listen, the rent's almost due. I think there are about eight hundred dollars' worth of other bills out front too."

See Dana sigh, next. "I'll put in a check on Monday."

Piero di Cosimo cross his mind some way last night? Fellow used to cower in the corner when it thundered.

So'd Caligula.

What time's Cornford get up? He anticipating he'll phone? Brightness fall from his tongue, will it?

Not about to find out. Springer'll no more than sip coffee and he'll be sweating like a spitted goat, cold's a virus.

Be dragooned for the next seventy-two hours, in fact, turn infernal on him. Bed's charnel, Dana exiled sexlessly to the couch. Consume her own weekend also, in and out medicining.

Pestilence. Hold him down to three or four vodkas a day, even.

Utilize the time to cultivate some answers. Soon's he can frame the questions.

Good gray versifier afford any wisdom? Springer'll task him in midweek, back room of the saloon. Grimy soporific afternoon, Pike's alone with club soda and a *Sporting News.*

"Lipp."

"Loosh."

"So. Name me ten men who played at least two decades in the major leagues, full career on only one team each."

"Hmm, pretty ingenious. We counting people like Ted, with the military time?"

"Encyclopedia says less than twenty."

"My blood's phlegmy. Walter Johnson? Stan the Man? Mel Ott? Luke Appling? Brooks?"

"That's five."

"Now it's coagulated. Who else?"

"Sit with it. Answer me something different instead."

"Ask."

"What the devil do you do when you're my age, wife, kids of ten and twelve, and all of a sudden you've got such a myopic dose of the hots that you can't piss straight?"

"*Oy, Gevalt.* Punt. Are you serious, you hypertrophic bastard?"

"Name the symptoms. No space for a damned thing else in my head."

"The girl feel the same way?"

"Verge of it. Seemed to be, anyhow. It's a week. I haven't had the guts to pick up the telephone since."

"Ah, me. What about at home?"

"When's that ever a factor? You know Dana, whose marriage could be better? Oh, yeah, the usual declension, inertia, things taken for granted. But still."

"Al Kaline do twenty full seasons?"

"Yes. That's six."

"Jesus, chum, I don't know what you want to hear. I

thought mine was all battened down for life too. Until Esther just decided *adiós*. They're precarious enough even without the Seventh Commandment."

Springer'll smile. "Tell you the truth I'm not quite certain how much Dana'd mind. Be the first time in living memory she'd seen me *reacting* to something."

"Sure. Lucien, she's great people. That great nobody ain't."

Pike'll ruminate into cigar smoke. Off the bottle for years, cigarettes recently also. Springer looking half a generation younger, shaggy Lipp'll chant dactyls over his grave.

"Matter of fact I'd be damned discreet about it. Especially if it might only be an extraneous hard-on."

"Lipp, I've had an extraneous hard-on every third night you've run into me in this place. This girl I think I'd like to start waking up to, mornings."

"*Kyrie eleison.* Do I know the damsel we're talking about, incidentally?"

"You just told me to be discreet."

"Meaning yes. Ah, Christ. Here sits the poet in perpetual oestrus, and still another's whisked out from under. You parsed the ironies in it, at least?"

"How not? Where do I get the *shekels* for my tab out front here, even? Propitious moment for a second childhood."

"Go predict the gonads. Ted Lyons on that list too? Cap Anson?"

"Both. You're impressive."

"Who're the others?"

"Mel Harder. Wait. Oh, Red Faber."

"Tough ones. Makes you wonder."

Springer'll scowl. "Wonder what?"

"How come practically every writer we know knows more about that kind of horseshit than about life?"

Fragonard Utrillo Caravaggio Kandinsky. Fabritius Uccello Cimabue Klee.

Newer diversion. Eschatological acrostics.

Ten days, is it now? He actually finally dialing?

"Hello?"

"Jessica, hi. It's Lucien Springer."

"Oh. Hi."

"How are you?"

"Good. How are you?"

"Rotten. Listen, I've wanted to call. Or write, at least. Something."

"Lucien, it's all right."

"It stinks. When can I see you?"

"Well, I'm busy tonight, if that's when you had in mind?"

"What about tomorrow?"

"I'm seeing a friend tomorrow too."

Fuseli Ugolino Canaletto Kline.

"Lucien? I really can't break either of them. I'm free Tuesday, though?"

"Same time okay?"

"Fine."

"Jess? Listen."

"Yes?"

"Oh, hell. Never mind. I'll see you then."

Sassetta Hals Ingres Titian.

4

"Dana Springer's office."

"It's Lucien, Ruth. She tied up?"

"Oh, hello. I don't think so. Hang on."

"Hi, my husband."

"Hi. Something I've kept forgetting. I ran into that girl Jessica Cornford for a minute one evening. Somehow I got myself decoyed into seeing her tonight."

"After dinner, I hope? I'd planned sweetbreads."

"Oh, sure. It's only her manuscript."

"God, I do wish you'd help me with some of those piled up in the bedroom."

"Come on, Dane. You know where my attention span is at, these days."

"I just don't ever seem to get an hour to myself."

"Well, listen. Instead of cooking. One night soon, we'll do dinner out."

"Lucien, there are four of us."

"On me."

"*Shlemiel*. There's my other phone."

Springer also considering flowers while he's at it here? Lilies of the field. Toil not, neither do they spin.

Nonplussed going in there. Girl's smile couldn't be warmer, however. Hands to her shoulders, he'll grasp and gaze.

"Old succubus Jessie."

"Am not. How have you been?"

"I started to say. Woeful. Defenestrated. Stercoraceous."

"Hallelujah. What does the last one mean?"

"Pertaining to shit."

That silvery laugh, all longing's resurgent anew.

"Jess? You do understand why I didn't call?"

"Lucien, I'm twenty-five. You aren't the first married man in my life. It's you who have to make your own decisions."

"I keep making them like Saint Augustine. Lord, let me stop fucking around. But not yet."

"That's not quite how he put it."

"Close enough. All I'm sure about is that I want to see you."

"Well, here you are. So will you stop looking so sulky? Anyway, come on. There's something I have to show you."

Bedroom's where she'll lead. Imprimatur on the latest clutter, she petitioning for? Corner closet's been sacked by Visigoths.

"*Nu?* This time your cleaning woman heard voices."

"Dummy. Just look, is all."

Sluggish on the uptake these weeks, won't reach him until she's assaying a *media-verónica* with a tan corduroy jump suit.

"Pernicious influence, what you are. Can you believe three of them?"

Creature's merry as a minnow. Recidivistic Lucien feeling any less so?

"*Olé*. Will you kindly tell me what I was doing away from here for so long? And will you also give me a rather immediate kiss?"

"No. Go sit. Let me try one on for you."

Bed be the handiest pew. While there comes that sacramental buttocks out of Jessica's jeans.

So much for vexatious theological irresolutions.

Beside him's naked Jessie again, Springer's come back from that faraway place. God o' mercy, how his innards get constricted.

"Oh, damn, Jess. Tell me what you've been doing?"

"Whining over that intractable manuscript, mostly. Or inventing excuses to avoid it."

"That's not what I'm talking about. Who have you seen?"

"Oh, friends. Your paramour Norma Miljus, one evening."

"I suspect I don't mean women."

Mirth there. "Well, Max, a couple of times. I told you about him."

"Max Kant. Max Fichte."

"That's sort of psychic. Idealism's what he mostly teaches. It's Max Nagel."

"Did you sleep with him?"

"I told you that too."

Hand near that mossy woodland of the elves, Springer has, Jessie'll aspirate a breath when it ventures the enchanted glen.

"I'll write him a term paper. If nobody's fucked it, can Jessica's twat exist? How can anybody be with you that often and not wind up babbling?"

"Oh, don't be gross. We're just close."

"Who else?"

"Do you know Adam Herschberger?"

"Seriously?" Political journalist Springer's saluted in briefest passage, craggy austerity he'll visualize here. "Isn't he pretty old?"

"It just seems so because he's been around so long. He's divorced. We have dinner."

"Any more?"

"Recently? Miles Tinning."

Solves that television news face from the saloon. Springer wishing this one a little less flaxen and manly, perhaps?

"You going to tell me you don't screw him either?"

"Well. I do. Sometimes."

"Come on. What does sometimes mean?"

"He's got a kind of sour marriage. Now and then all he wants is a sympathetic ear, really."

"What about this time?"

"Must you know?"

"What harm? Or for my mythical novel, say."

"Goose. Yes, I screwed Miles Tinning last week."

"He the only one since I saw you?"

"I think so. Yes."

"Oh, Christ. She *thinks* so."

Laughing while he'll kiss her at that. Fishified fingers up from below also, he'll usher them amidst their wallowy mouthing.

"Thus I refute Berkeley. Or wait. I just had a better idea."

Onto his hands and knees, Springer's scrabbling around to the bottom of the bed. Awesome perspective ever, those thighs primordial from here.

"Now what are you up to?"

"Philosophic masterstroke. Eat Jessica Cornford as the ultimate empirical proof of reality. *Cunnilingo, ergo sum.*"

"Oh, Lordy. Don't I get to philosophize too?"

"*Noli me tangere.* Concept's all mine."

Cornford's laughing. "Ah, well, I should worry. Sixty-eight, then?"

"Sixty-eight? What's sixty-eight?"

Shaking with it. "Oh, how delicious! You go down on me, and I'll owe you one."

[65]

Sorcery thereafter, headlong into lubricious delirium she'll spirit him. *Malleus Maleficarum*. Casuistical scoundrel named Urbain Grandier Springer's become, all the demoniac nuns of Loudun he's copulating with at once.

Witches' Sabbath, the blasphemy's endemic here. Swaddled in paroxysm's where she's got him next, he'll spiral through orgiastic ecstasies and ejaculate in tongues. Remind him to check for stigmata when he's back from the drowned.

Omophagic, only word for her labia. How's he even remember, means eating raw flesh? Springer's havocked.

"My God. *La Belle Dame sans Merci*. Inquisitors be after you."

"What did I do?"

"Black Mass. Jessica the depraved prioress."

"My chalice runneth over. With jism. How lovely, whatever."

"So why didn't you come?"

"Didn't I?"

"Stop it, now."

"Lucien, it doesn't matter. I was out of myself completely."

"Still."

"Believe me, it wasn't your fault in any case. I'm pretty sure I was holding something back."

"Jess?"

"Well. After what happened. When you didn't even phone."

"Oh, damn it, you know I wanted to. I was chewing furniture."

"I told you I understand that. But there's my side of it also. It probably wasn't even wholly conscious, but I did have to build some defenses."

"Oh, Christ."

"Don't be upset about it. Please? The next time will be fine."

Cleaved and pulsing still, Springer's lips'll purl at her sweated jugular. "The next time will be about two cigarettes from now."

"I wish. Not tonight, though."

"Says why?"

"My darned office. I have to catch a six o'clock plane to Washington with another editor. Senatorial breakfast, no less."

"Call in sick. Hoof and mouth disease."

"Be grateful for lesser dispensations. Anybody else, and I'd have postponed tonight altogether."

"Ah, me. Just have to write it off as the worst sexual experience of my life, then. Be able to describe it in a single word."

"Don't tease. Which?"

Continue to lick at that sensuous throat, Springer will, delighting.

"How's stupendous sound?"

"It just occurs to me that I can be companionable and recite Kant like your man Max myself. Watch. Two things fill me with ever-increasing wonder and awe. The starry heavens above me, and Jessica Cornford beneath."

"Go home."

"You be back by tomorrow evening?"

"Afternoon. But I'm having dinner with a girlfriend."

"What about Thursday?"

"I'm seeing a friend then too."

"That *f'shtunken* word. Bathsheba use it with that benighted Hittite, do you think? Can you get your own dinner tonight, Uriah? I'm meeting a friend."

"Go home."

Dressed but loath, so feline and stretchy's Jessie now. Flimsy nightgown she's undulated into. "Tell me what you're like in the morning?"

"Splenetic. Stercoraceous. Go."

Jonathan Hundley's accustomed. That urbane television *hombre*? Who other of late? Sense of investiture deepening for him, no question.

"Listen. I just remembered."

Squiggling onto her belly next, pillow's ensnared. "Unnn?"

"I'll find out which weekend. Dana and the kids are invited to Woodstock. Here's my plan. Uninterrupted debauch."

"Go home."

Lewdly hiked up's her nightie next, he'll lean and puckerishly anoint each gibbous cheek. Globuliferous epithalamium.

"I also forgot to tell you who my favorite painter's become. Used to fill his studio with badgers and ravens and Barbary apes and turtle doves. Among other indulgences. Name of Sodoma."

"Oh, Lucien, go."

Two more osculatory adorations first, moon by moon. Giddy Loosh. Any of those churlish Augustinian antinomies been disentangled here meanwhile, would he determine?

Be halfway to the saloon before he even recalls they broiled that reprobate Grandier at the stake.

Immortal spheres, O luscious pair,
I trust she rides thee not
Too harshly there. In silken sheets
Dost grace thy nights, and for thy days
Will virgin vestments wear, nor chafe,
Nor clump too cruel upon a chair.

Exotic orbs, sweet blossoms rare,
What other splendor canst compare
To thee, when thou dost flare
As boldly my encroachments dare?
Ah, *tush*, I trust she sits thee not
Uncushioned there!

Ah, *tush*, let gaudy trumpets blare
While others boast my lady's breast,
Her calf, nor can I care.
But shouldst my lady bid me share
Thy glory with another's stare,
O, globes! Despair!

Despair, alas, dear seat, sweet pair,
To think she'd use thee wanton there
And wipe me bare! How dump on him
Who dost eternal swear
'Tis what his lady dumpest *with*
He holds most fair!

10

Iamb, therefore I am. Wednesday safely neuter and past, so who's with his wandering wench tonight?

Mirabile dictu, female now also, back room of the saloon. Behold, Springer has heard that there is corn in Egypt.

"Lucien, hello!"

Radiant, no less, turn him mealy. Squeeze her elbow when he sits.

"Damn, you're beautiful."

"Behave. I don't think you've met Phoebe Cissell. Lucien Springer. Phoebe groans through life with me at the magazine."

Beeswax hair, chubby bright face. "How do you do, Lucien?"

"Hi. But I'm on my way out again if you're talking shop?"

"Bitching, is all. Pheeb just spent weeks making a silk purse out of an asinine assignment, and all the boss did when she handed it in was stare at her boobs."

Subject chauvinistic Springer's learned to skirt. Suspecting himself of an incipient smirk nonetheless, girl's triumphantly endowed.

"Lucien, it's not funny. It's a pain in the bottom."

Beaming at him still, however, this the Jessica supposed to be contriving defenses? Behave, she say? Hand at his thigh beneath the table now even, oh bless us every one.

"I think you'd better stop."

"Give me a reason."

"You'll see if I have to stand up."

Cissell seeming to read all this gaily. Girl dredging out dollars also, though?

"Hey? You're not letting me break up something?"

"I needed the excuse. Honestly. Let me leave you two adolescents alone."

Check waiting there since, actually. But still.

"It's all right." Cornford's amused. "Phoebe's been trying to shut me up for the last hour. I'll see you tomorrow, Ciss."

"If I even make a showing. Lucien, good meeting you."

"You too."

Long wreathy minute then, cut it with a knife. *Incroyable* what she does to him.

"Anyhow. Explain why you're glowing so."

"Too much time with the sun lamp, maybe. Just before I got here."

"Cunt. Supposed to say it's me."

Hand tightening to say it down below instead, any of Dana's sixty dearest friends two tables away? Who's Dana?

"You sure about her leaving that way?"

"Don't worry. She's also just edgy. She's seeing someone and it's not working. Is it only midnight?"

"Not even."

"Let's leave too. Can you? I was actually hoping you'd come by."

"You bought Vaseline?"

"No, prune." Laughing. "But if that's the only thing you can think about, what I have in mind is even better. In fact it may well be the most memorable orgasm of your life."

"Tell me, already."

Calculating cash of her own, grin's all smugness next. "And no alternatives this time either. My manuscript. All that's legible."

"Oh, you shifty slut."

Ars longa, sex sometimes.

"What's the proper form of address? All you cuddly members of the Swedish Academy?"

"What better? Go on."

"As I deign to accept this questionable and long overdue token of my genius—"

"Magnificent."

"Wait. I also find it incumbent upon myself to voice some few cliché-ridden words of gratitude to another American novelist without whose selfless wisdom I'd not stand here today."

"That's a thought, incidentally. Who'll get you dressed decently?"

"Piss off, you rent robes. Anyhow. Little did I myself comprehend, in my earliest purblind efforts, the extent to which I'd mucked up such seeming bagatelles as tone, structure, point of view—"

"Needs more rhetorical conceits. How about my palsied shaman's hand?"

"Oh, Lucien, it will work now, though. Fiction is just so new for me, I couldn't seem to step back and see it whole."

"It's fine, Jess. Can be. Parts of it are already."

"What I wouldn't give to quit the magazine and try it full time. Do you think my agent might be able to get me an advance if I really bring off the revisions?"

"Do it first, laureate."

"And why do I feel so bubbly? I'd almost like to start right this minute."

"Oh, now hell."

"What?"

"This minute's all of a sudden twenty to three. What are you doing tomorrow?"

"Something's sort of hanging. Call me, why don't you?"

"Typical, typical. But listen. The girl, Susanna. She a fantasy you?"

"Well. Remotely."

"So who are all those *pendejos* she's running from? Am I going to find out you've screwed the lot of them?"

"Creative enterprise, banana brain. Give me a kiss and go, if you have to."

"Ummm. How do I feel so good just standing here and holding you? There an almanac on one of those shelves?"

"Heavens. Why?"

"Who won the Stockholm thing for self-control last year, I wonder?"

That disheveled *vahine* look when the light's oblique,
Gauguin she once put him in mind of?

Dreamy morning's speculation in it. Springer's age to
the year when he packed off to Tahiti for fair.

Kurt, three grand. Fred, Maggie, Leo, Alex, Rusty,
Norman, two each. Willie and Lipp, one.

Come live with me and be my love.

Out of the office when he phones, won't raise her at home later either. Where's it leak away to so fast, all that heady juice?

Come sloshing right back. Saloon again.

Get him gushy with the romance of it even, selfsame spot where they plighted their troth. So to speak. "You hiding something, Jess? Kidney troubles?"

"My tutor, *wie geht's*?"

Lambent again also, Polynesia right here. Man landed syphilis anyhow.

"I was calling."

"Bleepy laundry and things. I'm in the back with Max."

Table in *The Last Supper*'s too small. Hands and feet on Michelangelo's *David* are too big. Max quotes Occam's razor and they don't hump.

"Would you believe I sat up until five o'clock rereading the whole manuscript? You're right about practically everything, I think."

"How's Max feel about it?"

"Now stop, I said I might be out. He's had problems with his ex-wife and he needed to talk."

Kissing him then, merrily chastising peck. "Sometimes you can be dopey. I swear."

All mimsy the borogoves therewith. Still, dialectic's a ballbreaker. How's she leave him so reassured and flayed at once?

Trickier conundrum. How's he about to sit this through?

Wasting in despair's how. Saturnine hour and fifteen before he'll pipe them passing. Man he'd noticed with her a month back, realizes, towheaded Ichabod Crane with glasses. Jessie clopping ahead.

Barest nod she'll offer, swallow half of his own good-bye in turn. Someone you know back there, Jessica? Looked contagious to me, Max.

Discourse on the Pre-Socratics tonight, Heraclitean flux. Can't dip your Diogenes into the same river twice.

Pair of her underdrawers flush in the center of the floor last night too, still there? Wipe the panes in his lantern before he lectures.

Mome raths outgrabe. Three A.M. and a stomach full of worms, Springer'll invest ten cents.

"Hello?"

"It's me."

Contemplating that, seems. Or's she having to wait while the wick's trimmed?

"I just felt like hearing your voice again."

"Lucien, I'm working."

"Max gone?"

"Yes."

"I was sitting here thinking about you. That can't be all bad."

"No. But be a little more trusting."

"Heck. I'm sorry. I'll call you."

"Good night."

Oh, Jess. Ring your bell in six minutes flat. Four. There to stay.

"Another vodka, Loosh?"

"I suppose."

Philosophy Is Such Sorrow.

14

Morning's splendiferous too. Kids screeching as an introit, Dana frazzled but coping. Cicatrice from an old tumor at her left breast over there, queasy hours during the biopsy he forget? Bowel-movement retrospection tuning out any of that golden-sands-and-crystal-brooks crap?

Couple more cigarettes, won't live to decide. Sixth hundred thousand, imbecile's well into. Gag on the toothpaste and hack up his *kishkas*.

"Good God, Lucien. Don't you think it's time to quit?"

"Anyway, I couldn't unless you did. I'd scrounge yours."

"That isn't fair, you know I enjoy the few I smoke. Would it help if I kept them hidden?"

"Now where could you put cigarettes around here so I couldn't find them?"

Possible to twist a sigh into a *double entendre?*

"How about inside your typewriter?"

Now Cornford's the one's ill. Springer's waited three or four days to call again, obscure principle there he'll eventually decode.

"What is it?"

"Promise you won't laugh. Every once in a while I get these low-grade infections. I mean vaginal."

"Did you go to a doctor?"

"Antibiotics. I'll be swell in a day or two."

"How do you feel otherwise? You in the mood for company?"

"Okay, sure. I was just being sort of lazyish and sprawly, in fact."

"Bring you anything?"

"Thine own scurrilous self. And wilderness were paradise enow. Oh, wait."

"What?"

"And a nice pungent Bermuda onion, maybe?"

Under the breadfruit tree again. This what she looks like sick, send a few bottles to Springer's other generals. Wrist at her forehead by way of his hello.

"I just took it. It's only one hundred or so."

"Get back into bed. Take that *shmata* off, though."

"What are you doing?"

"Be your guest. Sexless. In her sepulchre there by the sea."

"Necrophilia now too?"

"Like Dante Gabriel Rossetti, say. Buried all his poems when what's-her-name died, Elizabeth Siddal. Then dug her up again when he got itchy about publishing."

"He didn't really?"

"Fact. Besides which I've never seen you undressed in daylight before."

Feel it then, convective as they squirm and settle. Dear hot Jessie, roast through eternity like this indeed. Paolo and Francesca have some kick coming?

"Jess, Jess, Jess."

Noses bump, so close entwined. *"Oui, monsieur?"*

"Answer me what I'm supposed to do about you? I stayed away from the phone these few days deliberately."

"Lucien, let's try not to plan anything. You know I'm often busy anyway."

"Tell me news. No, tell me about Jonathan Hundley."

"I thought I did?"

"I mean about his wanting to marry you."

"Oh, well. It hovers."

"Let me make you an unwed mother while you're deciding."

"Wouldn't scan. I'd be spoiled rotten by all that child support." Smile defeasible there? "I had one not that long ago, do you know?"

"Hell. An abortion?"

"Pretty weepy, in a way. Cold winter nights, I'm sometimes still not sure."

"Tell me who he was."

"Someone I loved. It was already past reclaiming, he was jealous if I stopped to chat with the janitor. But he was kind to me when it happened."

So much unshared. "Poor Jess."

"I'm all right. Poor you."

"How?"

"That. You're bursting."

"Well don't make it worse, numskull."

Fondling's what she's about, she conceive how electric?

"I can't screw. Not for a few more days."

"I may just have to soliloquize. Like in who would fardels bear, when he himself might his coitus make."

"Heinous. Or does it make this your bare bodkin? Should I do it for you?"

"Turn over instead."

"Never. You won't get it in all over again. And I really did have a burning sensation the last time."

"Tiger, tiger. Just turn."

"Tell me what you're going to do?"

"Just lie flat. Oh, nuncle. I swear, it ought to be gilded or something."

"Not marble, nor the gilded fundament?"

"That's the girl I meant." Easing atop, Springer'll cranny himself along the cleavage. Cradled. "Reminds me. You never said if you got my last poem?"

"I got it. I'm doing an essay on its analogical tropologies."

"Whole thing's Biblical. What God told Moses."

"Rectal thermometers are more *kosher* than oral?"

"Close. And thou shalt see my back parts. But my face shalt not be seen. Lift up just a pica or so, let me get my hands under you. Ummm, scrumptious."

"Good grief."

"What's wrong with scrumptious? Euclidean too then. Whole center of gravity's down there in my hypotenuse. Listen, moan a little, will you?"

"Your square root? Why should I moan?"

"So I can recite. Where the whore moans, there moan I."

"Buffoon. Are you actually going to come that way?"

"Writing one more poem too. Happy Easter, dear keester."

"Impossible."

"Ummm. Speed the plow, it feeds all."

"Lucien, you won't."

"You keep a secret?"

"Tell me."

"I just am."

Gloppy coccyx, Springer'll tissue it dry for mirthful Jess.
"Lordy, the services I do perform. Drop by anytime."
"With charity for all."
"How about the last full measure of devotion?"
"Subtler by the minute. But anyway, listen. Enough with the sex *du jour*. Dana's going to make that Woodstock trip in about ten days. Save the whole weekend, will you?"
Teasing smile, what thinking? Bend to flick his tongue across her nearer nipple.
"Both nights, invalid. Dawdle over cheeseburgers even, be prodigal. You want me to make tea or anything now, by the way?"
"As a matter of fact I'm a little sleepy. All that strenuous carnality."
"You're the one with the dismantled crotch, Annabel. Go snooze, I'll leave you to your infirmities."
"Woe is me. And I forgot to ask the gynecologist if masturbating's allowable."
Ablutionary few licks be all, won't shower. "Ain't the era permissive, though. You guess someone like Mary Todd ever told old Abe she sometimes conscripted a finger into her own Emancipation Proclamation?"
Answer? Meant it, dozing already for true. Radiator's steamy, toga her lightly with the sheet. Handiwork of Callimachus, way it drapes.
Child one'd have with this creature indeed, sky full of portents at the nativity. Notion truly give him pause? Ah, Springer, whither the fuck goest all this?
Into the crapper belatedly goeth that tissue, icky with come. Eulogistic flush, he'll offer.
That these honored sperm might not have died in vain.

Young poet Dana's coddled's awarded a prestigious grant next day, wires roses. All her doing, card insists.

"Mother hen. Hey, I'm pleased for you."

"I only wish it were for something of yours. Lucien, aren't you ever going to get back to work?"

"Come on, Dane. Do you think I enjoy sitting around all day with a head full of straw?"

"Oh, I'm sorry. I've just been anxious lately, I guess. There always seem to be more expenses than I anticipate."

"Honey, I'll straighten out. Christ, I've got to or I'll crack up altogether."

"Are you sure you won't change your mind about Woodstock, at least? It's so unfair to Amy and Doak. You never do a thing with them."

"How can I with the mood I'm in? But listen. You take it the wrong way if I have a drink with that Jessica Cornford now and again?"

"What does that have to do with anything?"

"Just what we're talking about. She seems to be the only person I've discussed writing with at all recently. Maybe some of her enthusiasm will strike sparks."

"I'll send her roses like these."

All of the people some of the time.

Felicitous timing there, happens, seen leaving the saloon with her twice in the next few days. Be gossip.

Ironic for the moment, actually. First night scatterbrain's still feverish, Springer'll route her into bed and scram. Second time she'll be taking an hour's breather from the novel, pat or two on those immortal spheres and he'll let her get back to it.

Latter even bring him idly home with Dana still awake, compound the felony.

"Good heavens. Did they lose their license?"

Bed full of manuscript, she'll collate while he undresses. "You going to keep spending eighty hours a week on that stuff until you collapse?"

"You'll be well rested to take care of me."

"Thanks."

Curious realization with that, however, no real tiff here in weeks. Affair's taken the edge off his normal household testiness.

Surely. Revise that list next too, three recurrent great deceptions of contemporary culture. The check is in the mail. I promise I won't come in your mouth. Screwing Cornford's just the thing for Dana's nerves.

So why's he so bloody discommoded so often otherwise?

Girl's going obliviously on with her own bloody life's why, nary a hoot for Springer's private bloody *Weltschmerz*.

Pattern's elementary. With her, and he's whistling Puccini. Night like that one with gangling Max, hyenas at his guts.

Weekend'll epitomize the syndrome in spades. Dial thirty times, where the Jesus is Jessie?

Claude Lorraine was illiterate, trained as a pastry cook. Frans Hals was swozzled seven nights out of seven, wound up in an alms house. Uccello was simple-minded.

Oh, damn it, Jess, with whom?

Well beyond midnight Sunday. "Hello?"

Mazel tov. And how's he pulling off all this sprightliness, no less? "So. What have you been up to?"

Fucking that flaxen Miles Tinning again. Fucking that pontifical old fud Adam Herschberger. Fucking huddled masses of unnamed.

Jan Steen owned a brewery. What's she saying?

"Janet Stein, an old friend of the family. She's close to eighty, and I'd been remiss. And then tonight I went to the movies with Phoebe Cissell."

So giggly with relief he'll almost forget to put in a bid for Monday.

Oh Monday, sweet Monday! Where on the deck our Springer lies, while Cornford's giving head!

Oh gustatory Jess! Oh suctorial mouth! Oh labialization! Slurping and slurping in the widening gyre, genius at this, best alive.

Springer somewhere heard tell of it ever being bad, exactly?

No matter, deed's got him howling. On her hands and knees beside him, starry snatch above they once discuss? How long's he about to lie here supine and selfishly slaver?

Slither beneath, he will, there's the keen lad. Oh, don't stop though, ah yes. Now clutch those columnar thighs o'erhead, now wedge his kisser fierce betwixt.

Nose practically up her anus also, cataclysmic.

Be thou familiar but by no means vulgar, someone declaim? Give thy thoughts no *tongue*?

But oh breath, breath, breath, oh bleeding *soixante-neuf*! Where on the deck they both now lie, gasping, ah forsooth!

Whitman, thou shouldst be living at this hour.

Assault her newly, however, he'll gobble and knead and nibble and chomp. Armpits, navel, any succulent interstices he neglect?

"Oh, Lucien, make love to me now!"

Springer's so erect his cock's his quiddity. While how serpentine they'll wriggle as he (ah!) inserts.

All sinuous simultaneously her legs as well, oh Jess, their weld for perpetuity. Concupiscent madonna, her face beneath his, or's the oxymoron absurd?

And where's she guiding his nether hand, pray tell?

"Oh, Lucien. Ummm, so nice."

It was a lover and his lass. With a hey, and a ho, and a finger up her ass.

Marriage of true minds.

Eve. Aphrodite. Helen. Salome. Delilah. Isis. Nana. Beatrice Portinari. Iseult. Thaïs. Moll Flanders. Clytemnestra. Mary Magdalene. Catherine Earnshaw. Jocasta. Theresa of Avila. La Gioconda. Medea. Ninon de Lenclos. Garbo. Electra. Emma Bovary. Lesbia. Esther. Anne Hathaway. Carmen. Tosca. Circe. Isadora Duncan. Lady Brett. Galli-Curci. Nefertiti. La Pasionaria. Lola Montez. Mata Hari. Bernhardt. Ellen Terry. Pavlova. Dido. Cassandra. Theodora. Suzanne Valadon. Alma Mahler. Anna Livia Plurabelle. Simonetta Vespucci. Model for *The Rokeby Venus*. Model for Bernini's *Persephone*. Renoir's *Gabrielle*. Boucher's *Miss O'Murphy*. Eula Varner. Grushenka. Martha Graham. Callas. Jeanne Duval. Jeanne Hebuterne. Fernande Olivier. Dora Maar. Lou Andreas-Salomé. Fanny Brawne. Fanny Hill. Anna Magnani. Irene Papas. Dietrich. Becky Sharp. Ruth. Antigone. Penelope. Maud Gonne. Come into the garden, Maud. Jezebel. Phaedra. Pocahontas. Sacajawea. Hester Prynne. Maid Marian. Elaine the Fair. Kate Chopin. Jennie Jerome. Swift's Stella. Faust's Gretchen. Ibsen's Nora. Gertrude. Duse. Maggie, a girl of the streets. Bess, the landlord's black-eyed daughter. His own Maggie. Sara Monday. Joan Toast. Miss Frost. Dana. Temple Drake. Candace Compson. Margaret Drabble. Vanessa Redgrave. Jane. Fay Wray. The Lady of Elche. Lady Day. Lady Antonia Fraser. Lena Horne. Tom Jones's mother. Byron's sister. Pharaoh's wife. Lot's. The Wife of Bath. The Firth of Fife. The witches in *Macbeth*. The Loch Ness Monster. Birnam Wood. Dunsinane. Old Mother Hubbard. The cupboard. Little Miss Muffet. The tuffet. Little Bo-Peep.

The what? The who?

Ah, Lord. *Quel* fuck.

Archetypal.

So why in God's name'd he leave Jessie behind again? Last few moments and all's suddenly out of sync, this the third time?

"Oh, damn it, Jess, I'm sorry. Now I suppose I ought to lie here and yuk, or something."

"Lucien, it's still partly me. I'm still fighting it, I'm sure I am."

"*Merde.*"

"No, I must be. Everything was fine."

Wispy little kiss with that, eyes loving. Still.

"Oh, well, hell, we'll get it solved on the weekend. When we finally get some *time* together. Christ."

"Is any of it guilt, maybe?"

"Good question. It's never been much of a factor before."

"So I gather."

"What does that mean?"

Foxy grin there now. "Tell me about your night with Norma Miljus."

"Why? I thought I did anyhow?"

"Tell me."

"A sporting event, sort of. We were drunk as moths. She's pretty *zaftig*, but I half suspect we wound up trying wheelbarrows."

"Oh, how perfect. She called me, nosing around to find out if we were seeing each other. I said no, of course, we just talk a lot over there."

"And?"

"Promise you won't take it as any more than a joke. Not having an orgasm again reminded me."

"Will you come to the point, *Dummkopf*?"

"Well, if I happen to get interested, she'll let me in on something. You're some kind of phenomenon."

Soppy odalisque's his laughing Jessica next, shower with him tonight. Being proprietary about the soap, however, froth from her privates he'll purloin.

"What are you doing? Oh, here, let me."

Gobs of it into his hair, tub's too precarious for an escape. "Trollop. I was keeping it dry."

"Don't you think I've watched you, snaky?"

Haul her to him then, newness of her all sudsy and drenched. So achingly rainy her lashes too, seachange, when Jess was a tadpole and Lucien a fish. Lick riplets from her shoulder, neck he adores.

"Oh, Jessie. How do you always manage to make me feel so obscenely good?"

"Be nice and I'll even let you use my drier."

"Towel's faster. But that's just what I'm talking about, all this wingèd-chariot misery. God, I can't wait until Friday. Love you until your mechanism falls out."

So why's she looking at him like that?

"I might as well tell you now, I guess."

Oh, no. Oh, Jess, don't. Quick, names of all three Carracci, he able?

"Jonathan Hundley called this afternoon. He's coming in Wednesday, on business. He's going to stay through."

Earth receive a gimcrack guest, Lucien Springer's laid to rest. Annibale, Ludovico, Agostino. Stomach, be interred without.

"Lucien, I'm sorry. I wanted it myself, truly. But it's Jonathan, there's no way I could refuse him."

Agonía, scream do any good? Anything ever been resolved here, Springer in a position to assert any demands? Up to much more than coasting with it recently even, taking what he can get?

"Oh, hell, Jess, I know. There's hardly any breathless future in any of this for you."

So go see what being rational assuages. Naked Jessie meditative in the steamy fall, hair all darkly matted, can't even bear to look at her now.

"Lucien, I am sorry."

Sic transit gloria Monday.

"Gang aft a-gley."

"What did you say?"

"Not important. Best schemed lays of mice and so forth. Screw. Maybe I'll call Miljus, even."

"Why don't you? It might actually be wise, in some ways."

"I suppose. Or a new sort of phenomenon, at least."

"New how?"

"Every time she comes, I'll weep."

Not Miljus. Sultry quiff name of Beverly Allerdice, television actress. Been hanging, year or two. Walk her home same night Dana and the kids take off.

Girl's all over him in minutes also, ravening. Knees bony where he's just as precipitately up under her skirt, however, thighs thin.

Missing underpants capricious enough to compensate? Be wrist-deep before he thinks to question.

So what's this qualmish dull emptiness where he lives, meanwhile?

"Oh, damn. Wait."

"I know. I did have a bedroom, last I looked."

"No. That isn't what I meant. It won't be any good, Bev."

Pettish scowl there, prettiest of creatures in fact. Still clutching a rather incriminating refutation of what he's just announced, likewise.

"I didn't realize how late it is. Shit. One fast tumble and I'll have to split."

Dripping ingenuousness while he zips. "Let's wait. Until it's earlier, some evening. When it can be right."

Crediting this? Or's she reading him for addled? Lifetime of precisely such quickies, where's impulse fled?

"Soon. I'll call you, now. Good night, Beverly."

Avanti. With his cockle hat and his sandal shoon. Desolate and sick of an old passion, something like?

Call Dana too then, ought, even long-distance. Thrill to the capital fellow he's become.

Being faithful to Cornford.

"Hello?"

"Buenos días."

"Oh. Hi, Lucien."

"Your architect head back to Boston?"

"This morning."

"Anything on for tonight?"

"Well. I'm seeing a friend."

Bitch, times he despises her. Fucking well knows he's been masticating his own entrails the while.

"What about tomorrow?"

"Oh, dear."

Up thine, Cynara. Oh, Christ, realizes it's not purposeful either. Living her life as ordained again's all, how blame?

Irony even. Got the calls with Hundley in town, assumably, *maricones* not aware they were supposed to be off skulking.

Fat lot of consolation in the insight. He weasel enough to go groveling after thirds, now?

"Listen, I'll ring you later in the week."

"Do, Lucien. Please."

Spite his face.

Muddy-mettled rascal. All he needs, new reason to haunt the saloon.

Earlier than ever, yet. Dinner with someone like Phoebe Cissell, possibility.

Not, either night. Cloak of gloom he'll wrap himself into, remotest corner of the bar. Alone and palely loitering.

Oh, Jess, which of those spermatorrheal honchos this time? Can't stand it.

"Melancholy Lucien. Why do you look as if they just shot Emiliano Zapata?"

"Good Lord. Where did you come from?"

"Is there more than the one door? I had a short evening, an old girlfriend and her husband."

Practically titter at the reprieve again, actually come in here looking for him too? Glow at her. "Let me get you a drink."

"Well, I really just stopped by to cash a check."

Endless, endless, she have any hint the seesaw she's got him on? So where last night while he's back at the bottom then?

"On second thoughts I can cash it in the morning. There's a ton of wine at home, if you'd like to walk over?"

Guess. "You're incredible."

"How do you mean?"

"Never mind." Freshly filled vodka flush under his nose also. Was a vodka. "You all set?"

Give him that man that is not passion's slave.

"So. Did you set orgiastic bells ringing with my friend Norma?"

"Hell, Jess. I spent every dismal minute thinking about you."

"Lucien, I wish you wouldn't."

"Tell me how not. It's peculiar, though, somehow Jonathan Hundley doesn't bother me. Maybe because he's been a kind of *given* right from the start. What really chews me up is the idea of somebody new. Such as what did you do yesterday?"

"Adam Herschberger had called. I've told you, he's alone. We go to dinner."

"*Voilà*. The minute I know, it's wiped out. Almost."

Laughing. Trace of the weasel in him after all, however?

"Anyhow. Jonathan still talking about conjugal bliss?"

"Oh, not really. I do wonder, though."

"What?"

"Living alone. How do people screw around and then suddenly turn faithful? Would I have to make it understood that I might be recusant?"

"I could handle that with you, do you know?"

"Come on. I mean when there's real commitment."

"Nonetheless. And granted I'd crawl up a wall if I suspected Dana were diddling around. But in your case I'm at least partly toilet-trained already."

Sorting keys at her vestibule, uncozened Jessie'll view him awry.

"God, you're such a transparent liar."

Buss her cheek. Chain the fucksome fuckstress to the bed, likelihood of it.

"I'll tell you, though. I've got half an idea."

"Miraculous. What?"

Sprawled amid the low pillows opposite the couch, Jessie's whiskey head's at his hip.

"That moldy novel of mine that I'm never going to get back to. Toss out the whole misapprehended *megillah*."

"And?"

"Contrive one about Jessica Cornford. Those thousand unheeding misdemeanors she perpetrates on the person of helpless Lucien Springer, rather."

"Good grief, like which? I mean besides the sacrifice of her nubile ripe flesh?"

"Just now in the saloon, classic. There I am with visions of you accommodating battalions someplace. A minute later I'm almost ready to believe it's me you're looking for, so what do you say? 'I have to cash a check.'"

"Nerd. Don't you think it crossed my mind that you might be there?"

"Thanks. But it could still be a pretty comic concept, maybe. Or can't you have a protagonist turning pale and specter-thin at the age of forty-seven?"

"Why not? Fall upon the thorns of life too, say. Bleed all over the joint."

Laughing while Springer'll take her into his arms. Cathay, all's silken and magical in seconds.

"Oh, Jess, I just wish it were funny, though. Nothing else in my head ever, what it is is ludicrous."

"Now there's a compliment."

"Shit, you know what I mean. Wanting you so. And that weekend we didn't have. Except even if I could fake an excuse to get free for another one, I couldn't afford it. What an egregious mess I am."

"The unexamined life is not worth living." Laughing anew. "Listen, you're not. And even joking, this is the first time you've ever even obliquely mentioned the possibility of new work. Go ahead, immortalize me. I'll let you in on all sorts of murky secrets if you want. Like, oh, let's see. Bet you can't guess the very first merit badge I won in the Girl Scouts?"

"Poking your finger up when nobody else at the campfire could notice?"

"Better. Good grooming."

"Not possible."

"Was. Bet you won't believe how old I was when I lost my virginity, either."

"*Ora pro nobis.* Nine?"

"Two weeks before my fifteenth birthday. I'm a treasure trove."

"You may be. We going to live long enough for my pen to glean your teeming brain?"

"May be gleaning my teeming something else one of these days, just incidentally."

Lift where he's been lying across her, he hear that right?

"Which is why another bit of news is that I'm not going to sleep with you tonight, old pal, old stud, old soak."

"Oh, now hell. How late are you?"

"Eight or nine days. It might be nothing, that infection probably bollixed up my system. But it does dampen the ardor, you might say."

Considering her still. "That means you were due before Jonathan Hundley got here?"

"*Es verdad.*"

"Leaving me and Miles Tinning?"

"Sheats and Kelley. Less wild of my surmises says Springer. Oh, well, that's dumb to guess at."

Sigh be what follows, draw her close again. "Listen, I'm

going to get into bed with you anyway. Just hold you, for a while. Ah, Christ."

"What?"

"Didn't I already call it ludicrous? Right this minute I almost hope you are."

Pisser. Does.

Stout Cortez. Beauty is truth, truth beauty. Bird thou never wert.

Anything apply?

Map of her cavortings with the architect in topographical stains on the sheet, coital collage. Still peculiar, however, Springer's undismayed. Now's all, where curled to him newly's sleek esculent Jess.

"Strikes me. Contented this way, has to prove I do mean a lot of it. In my fashion."

"Jonathan's the same, sometimes. Just comforting physically, people need it more than they admit." Voice furry, face at his throat. "There's something I ought to tell you, I guess. About Wesley."

Knotting inside, new check's this? More, certainty. "That sounds promising. Do you suppose you should mention who Wesley is first?"

"The jealous one. The one I said I was in love with."

Vaguely. "Who was kind to you after your abortion?"

"Yes. Do you remember when I cried?"

"The second night I was here." Oh, doom. "Jessie?"

"He'd phoned. Just to chat. For the first time in months, that same afternoon."

Filippo Lippi once violated a nun. Trastevere trulls be whisked to Raphael on the Vatican scaffoldings, the more swiftly back to his brush. There some reasoned response she expects?

"It had been so lovely, Lucien. Both of our evenings. And then you were running away."

"Jess, don't I know? But what exactly are you telling me? Are you still in love with him?"

"I may be. He's the one who truly lingers."

"But you don't see him?"

"It's a year. No."

One whose child she'd wanted then also, what evoked him now.

Yet strange still, hers the hurt he's containing here after all. There anybody's definition of love would disanoint this?

Or of masochism's he mean? What more O Catiline? And how piquant's whatever exists for that coefficient Miles Tinning, by the coincidental way?

"Ontogeny recapitulates philogeny. You drowsy already?"

"Ummm. But this is nice. You are, Lucien."

"Anyway, there's some of it you can't make me share. In the saloon with Phoebe Cissell that time, when your hand was on my thigh. Just me alone. All of three whole minutes at least, tart."

Mumble to that, lost to their very closeness. Be asleep in no time as well, so fleet her escapings. Christ, like to stay, wake to this.

To what? Old horse Cornford, all he means in spite of all.

Ease out finally, however, though he'll lean anon. I kissed thee ere I covered thee. Mons veneris be where, seedling deep down things or no? Dearer with vulnerability either way, make her seem.

Cunty Jess. Curse her for being unkind while what's she ever but honest? And where any fabled rare offerings from peon Springer in turn?

Stealing a photograph of her, what he's up to now in fact, been lying about. Barelegged Jessie on a weathered rail fence, some further grieved dream she gazing off to there? Jonathan snap it? Very Wesley of her wistfulness?

Lacrimae rerum indeed, so fetching she looks. Be sore?

After all. Mother of his (and/or Tinning's) (maybe) child.

Five-and-dime frame, next noon. Common decency secret it from Dana. Common sense, more patent.

Photos all over his work corner, actually, Springer with other writers. Faulkner, old cummings, Dylan Thomas no less. Own name's writ in water, accumulating a closet fame vicariously.

Letting life accrete that way, starting to dawn.

He ever going to do a book again, truly? Even ceased agonizing over it lately, appears. Night with Maggie Oldring, last time he seriously felt the wrench?

Forty-seven, sainted Mother. Mute, inglorious Springer, season when he ought to be cresting. Calcified instead. Really possible he's turned out only one halfassed screenplay and three magazine pieces in four years?

Truer gauge of how gemlike's his flame. Never been asked to pose for Jill Krementz.

"I am Alexander, the great king." "I am Diogenes, the dog."

Billy Werber. Charlie Gehringer. Bobby Doerr. Eddie Miller. Frank Gustine. Johnny Pesky. Cecil Travis. Burgess Whitehead. Sibby Sisti. Kenny Keltner. George Kell.

Have it all to do over, be an aging infielder.

Be manic in another minute *también*, keep this up.

So what's attracting Cornford's misty gaze, there? She have him pegged, hot for young flesh the sum?

> Let not this praising of thy ass
> My deeper thirsts belie. . . .

Unwritten. Too dreary's his liturgy today, aware the whole thing's heading nowhere also, alas.

Wesley, now. Plus that sharecropper Tinning. Plus Jonathan H. Plus metaphysical Max. Plus Adam Herschberger.

Plus how much else unknown, what other rivals of his watch unzippered lurk?

And where any need for the burden of Springer on her own part, heap his fraudulent fey miseries on her doorstep?

"Ask any favor you will." "Get your *kvetching* royal *tuchas* out of my sunlight."

Still, still. Rip away her defenses, what he'd like, make her unlearn.

Y después? Cornford fall to her knees and forswear all others, just what would dashing young Werther here dare?

Leave Dana and the kids? Ever cast even the bleariest eye on that jolly proposition, somebody notice?

Arky Bysshe Vaughan, drowned in a lake. And Keats had tuberculosis like Red Schoendienst.

Anything he knows for sure besides the ache, finally? Feet on the typewriter, Jessie atilt beyond. Stare and brood.

And miss catching her at the office. No answer when he'll call from the saloon later either, naturally, dozen dialings between nine-fifteen and one-forty-five.

Keep an infant out, hour like this?

Oh, fool, jest and go mad. Where?

Bar conversation edifying, likewise. Town called Murcie in Queensland, learns, exotic potion habitually brewed from the koala. Imbibe it rank with surfacing bones and hair, however.

Say that again?

Koala tea of Murcie is not strained.

Cheerful as a sparrow the next A.M. "Hi, Lucien. *Qué tal?*"

"I guess I missed you last night."

"Oh, I had dinner with a friend."

James Abbott McNeill Whistler. Joseph Mallord William Turner. Jay Hanna (Dizzy) Dean.

Fishing, next. "You get any work done later?"

"It was Max. He's something of a gourmet, we cooked at his place."

Then sorted napkin rings until dawn.

"Anyway. Doting father, you might at least ask. I did get my period. I woke up to it after you were here, in fact."

"Makes me blue."

"I'm sure."

Put off a scholarly type like Max at least, would that? Or'd he read in Duns Scotus how to nose around down there and pull the string?

"Listen. I did a sneaky thing."

"Drank my bath oil. What?"

"That picture of you, next to the phonograph. I've got it framed."

"Do you honestly? What about Dana?"

"File cabinet. Though I may show it to her eventually. Research for my new novel."

"Lucien, there's no cause to rub her face in it."

"Would I? She knows you're someone whose head's a lot like mine, is all. But that reminds me, there's something in particular I want to talk about. You loose tonight?"

"I'm seeing a friend."

Oscar Fingal O'Flahertie Wills Wilde. Pissshit.

"Maybe I'll cancel that novel. Every third line out of the heroine's mouth be the same."

"Stop, now. It's just Adam Herschberger again."

Just. Again.

"He's been invited to a dinner party, Lucien. It's sad for him to have to go by himself."

"How much more of that before he proposes marriage?"

Oh, Christ, how much longer can this go on the way it is's the real question.

Can't. What he's got to see her about.

"How's tomorrow then? I do want to talk."

"Tomorrow's okay. Meantime I'd better shower and run. The usual time?"

"Or I'll call."

Take her to dinner for a change himself, why not? Whole town's supposedly abandoned intercourse anyway. Into Camembert instead.

Oh, *basta*, an end to jokes, can't bear any more of it. Got to quit, dying by chunks and pieces.

What'd Springer just say?

Renewed stimulation at the saloon that night too. Alice B. Toklas rampant with a hatchet, seems, but Gertrude'll take sanctuary in a grandfather clock. Niche in time saves Stein.

Sessions of his own simpering silent thought more salutary? All bony joints and trapezoidal angles, way he visualizes Max, copulate like a colicky giraffe. Gentleman-journalist Herschberger be black socks and garters to the indubitable end. Hairless calves also, wager.

Intolerable, intolerable. Himself, means. Girl's unblushing about the ones she does boff, why won't he take her word about the ones she says she doesn't?

Because yesterday's placid paramecium's tomorrow's slimy mermaid-fucker's why. Two-thirty's it gotten to be? Deep breath and Springer'll dial.

Third ring. "Hello?"

Sleep in her tone? Please, Jessie, yawn.

"Hello?"

Age forty-seven. Going on puberty. Hang it back same time she does.

Pigeons on the grass, how'd he fall into this anyway, wasn't Springer the stalwart always knew to elude slushy long affairs? Ambled over for the sport and wound up crippled.

Galactic chill, more akin, so deep's the longing. Call back? Screw the hour, go down?

Oh, Jess, tomorrow truly the last? I possibly mean that? How am I not going to see you?

Run off together instead? Now, soon, would she? Mexico, latest land of Cockaigne in his fantasies. Oh, darling, let's!

Girl happen to have a few unallocated *pesos* tucked away somewhere, maybe?

The devil, make do on *frijoles* and *arroz*, beans and rice. Matter? *Arroz* is *arroz* is *arroz*.

Shit for brains.

"Hi. Come in. Guess what happened?"

"I already know. Arrant degenerates ringing your phone in the middle of the night."

"Lucien, Lucien. He'd brought me home hours before. And hadn't stayed long either."

"*Mea culpa.* Anyway, what's your news?"

"Oh, exciting. I'm taking the next two weeks off. To work on the novel. Sixteen days, if you count the extra weekend."

"When did all this come about?"

"Impulse. I just haven't been getting enough done. And I don't have any exotic plans for the summer, really, so I simply decided to use half the time now. I called my parents in Ohio."

Unmentioned, undiscussed. So what's he to Hecuba that it had to be, alas?

"I suspect I'm glad. It connects with what I want to talk about, sort of. Makes it easier."

Questioning beside him on the couch, wretch also have to have the look of a Van der Weyden angel tonight? Glimmer of waist where her shirt's untucked as well, Max and Herschberger confront this same necromancy and do menus.

Springer about to say it? Must.

"*Merde.* I've got to stop seeing you, Jess. At least for a while."

Unlighted cigarette midway, gravely regardant. Or's it Van der Goes he means? One who went loony doing crucifixions, friars sang madrigals to keep the poor bastard at it.

Cf. Van Gogh, a nut by any other name. "I'm just

miserable, every waking minute. Like that call, I swear, I was half ready to flitch off an ear. Tormenting myself about the way things were at the beginning, mostly, dying to get that back between us. Except I'd probably wind up pissing and moaning like this all over again, with nothing ever defined still. And meantime I'm jealous of everybody you see, even your work, for Jesus' sake. The whole thing's finally idiotic."

"Lucien, it's hardly idiotic. You feel the way you feel."

"The way I feel is like rats' alley. The king my brother's wreck, whatever. Mistah Kurtz, he dead."

"It doesn't have to be like that. It could be lovely, if you'd let it. Lucien, I care about you. A great deal."

"Beautiful. So where does that lead us? We get to be friends?"

"Aren't we?"

"Come on, Jess. I'm talking about wanting you so much I could sob. Never having six unintermitted hours to *be* with you, take a simple walk on a simple afternoon down a simple street. And working out that bloody deteriorating sex mess also, just incidentally. Good Lord, go write about it. I'd sit there whimpering over the typewriter."

"I guess maybe it's a sensible idea, then."

"It's so sensible it sucks. It's just all there is, at least until I can get some distance on things. Oh, damn this."

Not answering now, pensive Jessica. Moment those breastworks were heaved up in anticipation of, presumably, what thinking?

"Anyway. At least the vacation gives me two weeks of rehearsal before the real affliction sets in. When will you go?"

"In the morning. I made a reservation right after I spoke to my mother."

"Maybe I'll write to you, try to get a handle on some of it that way. You mind?"

"Good grief. It's just Grasmere, Ohio, incidentally. General Delivery."

"Typifies the whole situation itself, doesn't it? So many commonest things I don't know about you."

"You know considerably more than most, in one cloacal area."

"Pursuing my spurious, self-indulgent sufferings, is all that's from."

"Still, I do wish you'd use some of it after all, if it would help. Get to work in spite of yourself."

"Yes, Dana."

"Stop. She's probably sick about it."

"You want to hear something funny?"

"Tell me."

"Dana, our first date. An hour after I got to her apartment we were in bed. No more than an hour or two after that we'd decided to get married."

"Oh, you're kidding? And it's lasted eighteen years?"

"Been in my mind, lately. Point is, you're the only one anything even remotely approximating that's ever happened with since."

"It makes Dana sound pretty darned remarkable." Laughing. "Or else like some sort of luckless martyr."

"*Tu madre.*"

"In any case, listen. Since you've told me where your head is at. Maybe I ought to remember that I have to pack. And I should make some calls, it's all so abrupt."

Van Eyck. Vermeer. Van Lingle Mungo.

"Lucien, is there much purpose in staying? Reasonably? And it's scarcely an auspicious night to go in there and screw."

"Oh, Christ, Jessie."

Clasp her to him, face at her neck. Being cruel to be kind, knows, for herself as well. But still. But still.

"Give yourself the time. Get the distance. You know I'll be ready to talk again when you want to."

Closer, cleave, beneath the ratty cherished shirt, dear bittersweet cherished allness of Cornford. No more of this? Of *this*?

And Mexico? Malcolm Lowry's, and the misericordes of unimaginable *cantinas* where sad-faced potters and legless beggars drink at dawn?

Oh, loss, impossible, how?

Hurry up please it's time.

"Jessie, Jessie. It's so fucked up. But I do love you so."

Standing, wracked, when'd they move to the door?

While gently at his throat's her lingering touch, eyes shimmering softly and wise. Press his hand onto a candle's flame next too, ah help, could. Oh, flee then, flee, get thee hence.

"*Ciao*, Lucien."

Jess Jess Jess Jess Jess. World's end, wail if he glances back.

Not with a bang but an elevator.

Hollowed be thy guts.

Part Three

1

But at least these sixteen days be manageable, that the supposition?

So what's he up to dialing Bedford Street at ten o'clock the first evening?

Gizzard rupture if it's answered. Not, means she did go.

Means she did if you're lucid. Stand there again come one-thirty, ring after ring after ring. .

Venial's all this is, however, so full of want's Springer. Or'll the incurable *nebbish* be at it tomorrow too?

"Hey, Loosh. You hear what they call a citizen of Warsaw with an IQ of more than ninety-five?"

"Must I?"

"Kike. Get it? Kike?"

"May I have another vodka here please, Mike?"

"Hey, Loosh. You hear about open admissions, everybody screaming for black studies? So they put in Swahili?"

"Unnn?"

"And the next semester they put in remedial Swahili?"

"Mike? When you've got a second back there?"

"Hey, Loosh, how long since you read Joyce? You hear what the newly amputated chef told Stephen's friend he was serving on the fancy silver platter?"

"Huh?"

"Plately stump, Buck Mulligan?"

"Oh, God. Mike?"

New favorite painter he'll finally nominate tonight as well. Pontormo. Kept corpses in a trough when he was conceiving his *Deluge*, sat around watching the bloat.

2

Ah Jess, Jess. . . .

If only we had been licensed to love one another! If only we had been free to grasp at our beginnings, to go, that swiftly, in that swift sweet sure first finding of each other that might have been, that almost was. . . .

And even now, still, should be walking hand in hand down our long lonely stretch of beach toward the sleepy, sun-scalded *adobe* hillside town beyond, to drink through the cloudless, wind-stilled late Zapotecan afternoon at a funky outdoor café we've discovered (and no one else has) where ragged barefoot children hawk ices in the white-washed cobblestone *zócalo* and ageless Indians nod by in the dusty wake of *burros* or goats, and then at night (oh Jess our nights, the night air!) the slow eternal wash and ebb of the sea. And in the mornings writing novels in our separate corners of the isolated tiny tin-roofed house we adore, hearing each other's machines and the mutterings and bangings-about when the work will not go well, the glorious unspeakable private silences when it will. And then again the long meandering lazy ever-beckoning walk (hand in hand) with only the surf and the wheeling gulls in accompaniment, even that irrepressible mindless prattle of new love diminished now in this uncanny bright sea-spawned miracle of our days, needing no words at all finally (though touching, ever touching, hand in hand) and no one else, our sandy sea-gleaming alabaster peace, so simple, so rare, so sane. . . .

Ah, horse, forgive. Buffalo Lucien's defunct, no help for it. Can it be possible he used to ride a watersmooth-silver vodka glass and break onetwothreefourfive Jess Cornfords just like that?

Jesus. Handsome mthrfckr too, was.

Write nice. As meanwhile I ponder via what diabolical and/or calamitous alchemy I am expected to remand these potted musings to the scullery of past tense.

Missing you. (Euphemism for extreme unction imminent.)

L.

3

Stately, hirsute Lippman Pike. Customary postmeridian far corner of the back room, man'll meet his Maker with that *Sporting News* in hand.

Gets his work out, however, more than can be said for certain other spavined plebeians Springer's not about to start naming.

"So, Lipp?"

"So. How did we sidle into a new season and no bets?"

"Lay me twenty dollars to five. Rod Carew's batting average and Nolan Ryan's strikeout total will add up to more than seven hundred."

"Hmmm, neat innovation. Make it thirty-five to a ten."

"Done. Barring sore arms and sprung tendons and such."

"Speaking of which. You haven't been mentioning that avocational bursitis of your own lately?"

"Fucking fiasco, is probably why."

Abstemious Pike'll sip soda, attending.

"Green-eyed monster, among other quotidian joys. From when I went skunking off, back at the start. She'd locked some drawers. Shit, how not, what future? Except now I wait in line."

"They also serve. Isn't it sort of safer that way? Settle for the *shtupping* and count your blessings."

"If I could stand it, sure."

"Maybe you'd better, buddy. I presume you're aware there's talk around? It is Jessica Cornford?"

"Ah, well, no great sweat. Dana knows we see each other anyhow."

All furrows, the versifier. "You want to give me that again? With maybe an anagogic footnote or two?"

"Spiritual. The girl's writing a novel. We discuss the ineluctable modalities. Agenbite of inwit."

"Springer, you are out of your suicidal mind."

Lengthy sigh almost instanter, however, he'll go on. "Then again. I did take a libidinous second look once I found out. How old was I, around forty, before I acknowledged that life wasn't a fountain?"

Springer'll wait smiling.

"I just hope I've got a few more years before I also decide a man can't build a case for a fanny like that one."

.... and in the mornings, they swim. Awakening, they will lie first in one another's arms, perhaps making love, perhaps not, but simply happy in each other, whispering there, or secretly amused, like children. And then, naked (for there is no one living within a mile) and laughing still they will race down to the water. . . .

Hair matted at her breasts, taste of salt upon her lips. . . .

And then their work, separately, in their separate rooms, separate machines clattering, or often the private silences. They read nothing of one another's until one or the other is ready, and then when it is by chance too soon, is a mistake and wounds are opened, then a sullenness follows (for they care about their work more than for each other perhaps, understanding that, and can be wounded terribly there) and that afternoon the walk along the beach might be solitary, one of them alone and yet full of the other and the pain of the moment's loss, as the victim sulks or perhaps recasts a passage yet again. Or perhaps, that one door still closed, they will both forgo the endearing town for that day, the sunny *cantina* and its few listing tables outside, the barefoot youngsters and the roosting fowl and the goats. One can all but abide the other now, he her, or she him, because of the task defiled, the instincts and the craft repudiated, until suddenly, miraculously, the faulted pages do perhaps begin to reveal themselves, the lines come uncaulked and it is possible that he was partly right after all, or she not wholly wrong . . . and then it is sunset on the deepening Mexique sea, the tiny faraway fishing boats flecked golden at the horizon, the heat lifting too and his arm goes about her and there are no words but this is a different silence now, ineffable and sweet and lorn, because this is their night, their life together, and tomorrow they will walk that long lonely sea-gleaming beach together, he and she, will work again and laugh again and will love. . . .

Hair matted at her breasts, glutenous purple prose oozing out of her ears. . . .

Ah, Jess. Aw, hell.

L.

What he needs is a herniary jugulating extravasational Marion-Tweedy-ish new piece of arse's what he needs is what.

Norma Miljus again? Third time he'll spot her in the two weeks. Buttressed bum and buttery boobs, recalls, acres of supplest forage. Requiting wench as well, what's to fear?

Come-hithering hi from Beverly Allerdice also, saloon's aswim in aloneness, third of a nation ill-fondled and ill-humped.

Won't, won't. Toss the drunken dog one bone named Cornford, lifetime's Pavlovian dedication down the stews.

A child said, *What is the ass?* fetching it to him with full hands.

Final scrotumtightening image as her elevator swallowed him, altarwise by owl-light in her doorway framed. A grief ago.

Imagining Ohio also, house on a hill. Dappled things, for Christ's sake? And brinded cows?

Ein Jessbetrunkener Mensch. Small rain down, forgot in his letters.

Pontormo at the bloated grange, pick his favorite ballplayer now too. Pistol Pete Reiser, ran into walls.

Anybody else in this feculent saloon aware the royalties from Gerard Manley Hopkins go to the Society of Jesus? Or that sculptured Dylan is twenty-two years of stone?

Christ that his Jess were in his arms, and he in that mangy bed again!

Blolly Moom. Night's last pour, Mike just proclaiming? While what's blathering Benedictus been doodling about?

> How uply screwed's the knot
> Of love that not now screws.

Un-crotched, must self abuse?
(If his is whose she'd not
Now use, since cannot knot?)

And how do you like your pie-eyed boy, Mistress Muse?
God bless President Roosevelt.

"What's with your girlfriend, by the way? It seems a while since you've mentioned her."

"Dana, she's not my girlfriend."

"I was only joking, for heaven's sake."

"As a matter of fact she's been away on vacation for a couple of weeks. There's a photograph of her in the bottom drawer there, if you're that interested?"

Eyebrow arched. And why the bejesus'd he spring that, exactly?

"Just an appealing shot she had extra copies of. I was supposed to hang it next to Faulkner for her, bring her luck."

Tender it, inescapable. Springer about to endure what they had to remedy Custer for, when the berserk Sioux squaw named Aggie Witt left teethmarks in his backside?

Briefest glance, he'll note first, speculation'd appear detached. "I was prettier."

Injun bite of Ag Witt.

Meantime a farewell to japery. As to *desultory* moping. Cornford due at her office *mañana*.

Late, let her get back. And not at the damned saloon. Please.

Be tripping over his own shadow in here from now on anyhow, knows. Half a dozen short novels dissipated this way already, has he? Ten-volume critical biography of Christopher Lehmann-Haupt go unwritten next.

Oh Jessie if you're home what doing, where?

Calling Max, oh the spiffiest time, how's every little Epicurean thing? Calling Adam Herschberger, Miles Tinning, Jonathan, Wesley, check in with the whole scrofulous world.

Only time she's ever called Springer's when he's caught her jammed at the magazine, okay if I get back to you soon?

Bien, understood, if a woman answers hang up.

Still, still, knows the saloon's listed, *bicho* contraption rings forty times an hour.

"Joe Flaherty, telephone!"

"Lipp Pike not here tonight?"

"Fred Exley, pick up!"

"Ted Hoagland just leave?"

"Vine Deloria supposed to be in town?"

"Larry Ritter or Don Honig out in back?"

"Joel Oppenheimer!"

"Bill Sheed!"

"Mike Harrington!"

"Pete Hamill!"

"Jack Mehoff! Jack Mehoff! Oh, I'll de-ball the next cocksucker who tricks me into yelling that!"

Bloodshot eye on the coin box too, anything be catastrophic in a chatty hello on his own part, how are things in Labia Minora?

Brake, brake. Gird up thy loins now like a man.

Phuck the phones?

"Hey, Loosh, you want to grab this?"

For him? For Springer? Oh, sweetheart! Oh my wondrous girl!

"Loosh? Listen, can we maybe cancel that bet? Be cultural schizophrenia if I have to root a full season against Rod Carew."

Antidisestablishmentarianism. What's all this?

"I just this instant found out. His wife is Jewish. He's actually taken instruction and converted."

By the rivers of Babylon, there we sat down, yea, we wept.

Jordaens Eakins Signorelli Seurat Ingres Carpaccio Ammanati.

Janáček Elgar Schubert Sibelius Ives Chopin Albinoni.

Jaspers Epictetus Schopenhauer Santayana Inge Condorcet Anaxagoras.

Jarry Euripides Seneca Strindberg Ibsen Calderón Anouilh.

Jerome Erasmus Schweitzer Savanarola Ignatius Calvin Anselm.

Joshua Ezekiel Solomon Samson Isaiah Cain Abednego.

Jupiter Endymion Sisyphus Scylla Ixion Cerberus Apollo.

Juliet Enobarbus Shylock Shallow Iago Cordelia Ariel.

Jakucki Embree Spooner Sundra Iott Cecil Albosta.

"Hey, Dad, can I borrow your scissors?"

"Dad, may I have a dollar for graph paper?"

"Jesus, will you guys ever be old enough to understand what my work is all about? Can't you see I'm *thinking*?"

Worst week of his life. Give or take a time when Dana once threw him out. No, that was worse. Kids small and precious, compounded it.

Not the kids. Dane. Christ, how he bled.

Lesson there, if Springer's possessed of the wit to grasp it?

No help. Cornford's all he can think about.

Dialing again too, hours when she'll be at the magazine. Hear it ring in the emptiness, who there since?

Oh, Jess, so ache to hold you, be *wrapped* once more.

Could have dropped dead in Ohio as well, anybody know to call him? Miljus? Cissell? Girl ever said two words?

And why's his own start jangling only when he's in the can?

"Hello?"

"Ummm. Lover of mine."

Not. Who then this throaty?

"Darling. Cat got your tongue?"

"Rebecca of Sunnybrook Farm. The Duchess of Medina Sidonia."

Laughter, carol back into register. "Asshole."

"For crying out loud. How are you?"

"How am I ever? Beset by the Eumenides. Or doing those cockamamie readings and being groped by flatulent academics. Tonight will be a full moon, or don't you remember I get summoned?"

"Full something else already, you sound like. What are you into, up there?"

"Scotland's blended best. Balm for this dark Friday noon-time of the soul. Or for the vertebrae. As a matter of fact I fell down a flight of stairs."

"Maggie, just what are you jabbering about?"

"I did. In Baltimore dunghill Maryland. I was fornicating with Poe's ghost. We went *tush* over martini glass."

"Is this serious?"

"Ah, Spring. Never believe me about anything, my eternal repository of denial."

"Will you quit the crap and tell me what happened?"

"I already have. God, I think it was a mile down. I seem to have this spine."

"And?"

"Nothing. I keep getting groped there too, but they wind up shrugging. That's what I called about, in fact. I've got a two o'clock appointment at St. Vincent's. And Arnold's away. It's so near, I thought you might meet me?" Sexy anew. "And then, too. Who knows what music might be heard?"

"Oh, shit, Mag." Sit there beforehand, sit again when she's inside. Looking to drizzle, likewise. "I can't."

"I really hate going alone."

"Hell, you know me. Nineteen days out of twenty I'd be telling beads. Today I'm just stuck."

"Oh, well."

Picasso Rubens Isenbrandt Courbet Kokoschka.

"I'm sorry. Really. I'll give you a shout tomorrow."

"No you won't."

"Go on, twat."

Hic jacet. Nugatory bastard, he truly so discalced he can't face half a dozen blocks, one measly hour?

Arnold not here, uptown with her afterward, even. Lay of his first minstrel.

Or'd all impulse be shot there too, while Cornford's meanwhile munificently screwing whom?

Ring back near six o'clock at least, token penance.

"Mag? Me."

"Spring, Spring. Let me down as always."

[*129*]

"It's your bum prosody. Anyhow, what did they say?"

"Try warm baths. Avoid disgruntled novelists."

"Be straight."

"I am. I'm a caducean bafflement. It's probably just change of life, or something."

"You should live that long."

"There's a fact. First sign of a hot flash and I'll take the pipe. Head into the oven."

"It's been done."

"I'm enviously aware. She was my age exactly, do you know? We once almost got into correspondence."

"Listen. Take care of yourself."

Sense something later. One he could still bed after all. Then lie furled into her easy lemony wet and tell her about Jess.

Listen too, Mag would. Call him a sad dumb fuck, most like, but hold him well the while, old Oldring.

Dial again, go up tonight?

Oh, Maggie, want the girl so.

Usual vigil at the saloon instead, naturally. Scrawl a surreptitious check for twenty, poke his mitered head in on Dana for the day's second moment's charity before he scrams.

"Damn, I wish you wouldn't work so hard on that drivel. I'll see you later, eh?"

"I'll be asleep. Wondering where we find the money for you to get there this early and stay as late as you do."

"Dane, I've been nursing them. Mike sets up a lot on the house, also."

"Your cup runneth over."

And surely goodness and mercy shall follow him all the days of his life?

Q. Springer's the one made the decision not to see her, why's he rooted here nightly with nothing but seeing her in mind?

A. Man is born free, and everywhere he is in chains.

Combat it at least modestly tonight, down half his first vodka before he'll deign to check the rear. Even hum Vivaldi as he goes. Or's that Haydn?

Dead and gone. But his memory lingers. On.

While across the room's Cornford. While across the room at a table with two men's Cornford.

Strangers both. And the faintest nod from Jessie's all, meaning what, dear Allah? Two with her not supposed to notice?

He crossing nonetheless? Insects in his ileum, where'd he ever learn Vivaldi had red hair? So heartbreakingly lovely, oh Jess. Crossing.

"Hello, Jessica."

"Oh, hi."

Muck Bulligan. And someone stole dead Haydn's skull.

"So. How was Ohio?"

"Good. I enjoyed it."

"You get some work done?"

"Scads. I'm proud of myself."

How beautiful thy feet in banalities. Hover fecklessly a week here, she make introductions even then? Oh, help, what is all this?

"Well. Maybe I'll give you a call, I'd like to hear where you're at."

"All right."

Sprucien Linger. Worm his way back out, whole abdomen's larval now. *Fuit Ilium.*

Who, who? He get a look at either of them, even?

Staying too? He plan on staying?

Will. Wait sniveling until she heads to the latrine, line up for crumbs.

Cunt. Peshitta-beshitting cunt.

Isn't, isn't. Positive she'll duck out here deliberately, must. Has to realize what he's gone through, Jess, Jess, it's three full weeks!

Jonathan Hundley one of them, that possibly explain? Safe old Max, why couldn't one have been? Same silent nod and Springer'd have strolled on, sane. Even recognizable Miles Tinning whom she fucks/sucks/takes it in the clavier from, suite be more tempered.

Oh Cornford in the name of the great polyphonic pessary will you come and please pee?

"Hey, Loosh, you heard about the new Warsaw bank?"

"Lester, I come to this place to drink."

"Bring in a toaster and they give you five hundred dollars."

"Go away, Lester."

Signal Mike for a renewal, eye fixed to the archway still. New affair with one of them? Getting married, anybody leap to tell him if that happened either? Can't be, can't, girl'd have called, sought him out first, would. Oh, lunacy.

Saloon plaguy with its own fractured dementia as well, now what's this beside him?

"Damn it, Phyllis! That still doesn't justify five nights a week in a massage parlor, where's your self-respect?"

"John, I've told you. I fuck better than I type and that's all there is to it."

Workers of the world. Young man Karl Buncular. Did spend those first two weeks on the novel though, seems. But what, how, so sudden since?

Oh, Jess, *miserere mei.* Hand in hand, aren't we ever then going to walk?

Or whose hand at his elbow next rather, what *tsuris* more?

"Listen. Can we go somewhere else for a while?"

Stare at her, brain may warp completely now.

"I told them I had an appointment. So we obviously can't stay on here."

Warped, is. "Jess?"

"Oh, heavens, Lucien. They're two journalism graduates I promised a friend I'd talk to. I would have been embarrassed if you'd had to sit there, they were so dull. Shall we?"

Q. Up with just how much of this can a man put?

A. From each according to his abilities, to each according to his needs.

"Hey. How have you been? Really?"

"Fine. And I did work. In fact I'll have a whole new draft of those opening chapters soon."

"You'll leave me jealous."

"Not very likely. Though I do think they're forever ahead of where they were. I'm indebted to you, Lucien. Almost everything you said was helpful."

"Hell."

"No, I mean it. But listen, never mind that." Walking, Cornford'll pause in perusal. "The question is how are *you*?"

"In dubious battle. At least I managed not to call all week, whatever that proves."

"Willpower of a saint."

"Saint Mary of Egypt, be about the only one."

"Who was Saint Mary of Egypt?"

"This hooker who went on some pilgrimage or other. Ostensibly on a pilgrimage. Mainly it made her the only female among about three hundred men."

"Since when do you get sainted for screwing?"

"Later. Contrition in the wilderness, or whatever. She started floating when she prayed."

"Because she couldn't get down on her knees any longer?"

Amused. They charted toward Bedford Street? Evidently.

"Anyhow. Did you get that Mexican stuff, by the way? Those two letters?"

"Oh, yes."

"Reread them now and again, would you? Let me pre-empt that one corner of your imagination, say."

"I won't have to, it's vivid enough as is. In fact I suspect I *could* go somewhere like that with you, do you know?"

"Sweet Jesus. Exactly what is that supposed to mean?"

"Dummy, I'm not suggesting it. I'm simply guessing that we could probably abide each other." Grin there. "If you'd let me work?"

"I wrote that in. Separate rooms."

"Lordy, all the enticing dreams, though. Do you ever stop to wonder what any of us are going to be when we grow up?"

At her entrance, Jessie'll unlatch. What to follow, Springer stopping to wonder about that either? Elevatoring.

"I hope you know there'd be even stricter rules about other things?"

"Such as?"

"Last week's brassiere in the kitchen sink."

"Stick to your own neurotic closet then, pal."

Hands firmly at her shoulders when they're in, Springer'll confront old Jess a minute. *Déjà vu*, almost feel like?

Even to the garlic. "Incidentally. Hello."

Puckered playfully, though she'll ease aside. "Bodily functions. *Pardonnez-moi*."

Follow idly bedroomward, john door only halfway swung. "Nor wonder where I lost my wits. Oh, Caelia, Caelia, Caelia shits."

"What's all that?"

"Nothing. Poor buttocks-offended Swift. God almighty, Jess, you really are something."

"What, what?"

"Pristine's one thing. But who else would still be living out of her suitcase after a full week?"

Coin a word, creature demands. Strewage? Bed the usual shambles too, oh Christ, worse, monochrome Pollock in the sheet-drippings this time. Saturnalia here, who?

Flush she's emerging upon, skirt hiked and adjusting panties. Home to his thigh-borne ills Springer's returned,

[135]

odi et amo as she downward smooths. He asking? Gaily even, watch him pretend.

"So. How many times have you gotten laid since you came back?"

All innocence in the moment's contemplation, no less. "Once, actually, since you ask."

Murther, murther, he plunging on? Seems, seems, impale himself altogether.

"Any good?"

"As a matter of fact it was, sort of."

Dies Springer. "Tell me who it was."

"Now don't be silly. I've got to be discreet about people, Lucien. I'd protect you the same way."

"Who wants protection? Tack up an announcement in the saloon, see if I don't stand there snickering."

"Simpleton. You would."

Insides inspissating still, however. "Tell me if it was somebody new, at least."

"What difference does it make?"

"Ego. Being cut in on. Who knows?"

"Lucien, there's been nobody new since I met you." Twinkle therewith. "And not enough of you *or* the few others, to tell the terrible masturbatory truth."

Laughing in spite of himself, clasp her where she'll glide merrily into his offered embrace.

"Damn you sometimes, Cornford."

"Dodo. I do have normal physiological urgings. Though they scarcely turn me into Saint What's-her-face."

Holding her, here's that meld. Bed's just behind them, here's all alexin of his cure as well. Cure or kill, means, now hell, now hell, they about to fall into this so readily anew?

Arms at his neck and gazing's his gorgeous Jessie next, no words, though Springer's seeing singing in her eyes.

Are.

[*136*]

Synaxarion: St. Lucien the Apostate of Washington Square.

Humanist, mystic, theologian, ascetic, mendicant, visionary, martyr.

B. New York (U.S.) *ca.* 1928. Libertine and philanderer who underwent sudden conversion in Bedford Street (*aetat.* 47) and lived a solitary life of penitence for three weeks thereafter.

Subsequently floated when fucking.

"*Merde, merde, merde, merde, merde, merde.*"

"Lucien, don't worry about it."

"Come on. You didn't even get started."

"I guess it was pretty fast."

"And it's not about to change either. Not until we get some time together. By now I'm anxious enough so that I half anticipated it before it was happening."

"You do drink too much, you know."

"Oh, Christ. Is it only eleven? Let's see what comes of it later."

"All right. But stay inside me now."

"I will."

"Anyhow, it's still partly my fault too."

"Not tonight it wasn't."

"But I do hold back. Even wanting you I sense it."

"God, I wish we could begin over again."

"Lucien, how? Listen, you called me once, and while we were talking you answered a question from one of your children. Don't you think that does something to me?"

"Oh, damn this all."

"Anyway. Why don't we change the subject? Guess what I just realized?"

"What did you just realize?"

"I'll have a birthday in a while. Why should twenty-six seem like a milestone?"

"Certified spinsterhood. Tell me what you'd like. That doesn't cost more than fifty cents."

"A baby, I think."

"Are you serious?"

"It does cross my mind. Since long before you brought it up, actually."

"Would you have one without being married?"

"I've thought about it. It would mean an end to my Emily Brontë fantasies for a while. Among other sundry divertissements."

"I am going to write about you, I suspect."

"Tell me."

"It may be simmering a little. First time I've had the feeling in so long I can't be sure."

"Gosh, I wish you would. Write *something*. Do you know me well enough? Even as a point of departure?"

"It wouldn't essentially be you anyhow. What I said that last time, the poor attenuated slob who has to endure it all."

"Oh, stop."

"I mean it. For vexation killeth the foolish man, and jealousy slayeth the silly one."

"Lucien, you're hardly Job."

"Nonetheless. Take tonight, when you didn't introduce me. Within fifteen seconds I was convinced you were running off to Arabia Deserta with one of them."

"Oh, glory. I'm sorry."

"It's nothing. Now, once I'm with you again. Right this minute I don't even care who your other hump was this week."

"Stop reaching. I'm not going to tell you."

"How do I do the book?"

"You just said the protagonist suffers. Let him, it's good for the pancreas."

"On the other hand there really is one fairly insurmountable problem."

"You've forgotten which end of the pencil works?"

"How do you write about something when it's still going on?"

"Drip. Are you talking about a novel or an autobiography? Break up his marriage, why not? Send them to Mexico after all."

"When push comes to shove he just might be too bourgeois."

"Or insolvent, in any case."

"Cheap shot, woman."

"I'm teasing."

"Keep at it and I may decide to kill you off. I might anyway. Yet she must die, else she'll betray more men."

"Trite. At least be ironic instead. Suppose he puts an end to the affair because of guilt, say, and then he finds out his wife has been updating Krafft-Ebing with someone else all the while?"

"And whenever it lags I'll toss in a knock on the garret door. Then in strides a personage who is a stranger to all present."

"*Nyet*, Fyodor. But get started anyhow, why not? Won't you discover where it's headed more quickly once you're sitting there?"

"I already do know one thing."

"What's that?"

"The theme. Just from the feel of your thighs alone. Be the same as in *Moby Dick*."

"Oh, now for heaven's sake, how?"

"Captain Ahab. One pair like these in Nantucket and he'd have stayed home nights."

Beasting with two backs again, Springer and this genie
who transports him so. So rendingly beautiful beneath him
too, ravaged *sfumato* features in these moments like old
tempera scarred, stab through him when he'll look. Yet
why's he so embattled here, why can't he contrive to make
her come?

So cautious he'll ply this time, all bridegroom anxiety's
Springer, in Priapean prayer beseeching that Jessie'll come.

Oh Vishnu, make her come. Oh Mithra, make her come.
Oh Avalokiteshvara, make her come.

Oh Jessie heart please let me make you come.

While so belongingly paramour'd they remain for all
that, Jess upwedging at him there, mortise and tenon till
her very matrix he'll finally probe. Ream, oh again, ream,
jewel in the lotus, is. Womb wending and afloat anew, under
the Bo-tree's Springer, mounting Pisgah's Springer, almosting nirvana's Springer, oh spumescent Wotan, yes, oh suc-
tionish Zoroaster, Springer once conceive eternity as this?
Thrusting forever in the Jessican depths?

But can't, but can't. "Oh, Jess. Wait. Give me your
hand."

"What? Where?"

"Here."

Losing his erection's the tragicomedy now, ring Jessie's
fingers round to remedy it back. Working? Oh, no, oh
prurient Christ, he ejaculating?

Oh diabolism, is! Oh damn, oh hell, oh help!

"Shit, shit, shit, shit, shit, shit, shit!"

Loss, loss.

Jetsam then, and Jessie the draining tide, he'll wish he
could disappear.

Om mani padme hum. Ignominy.

"I'm sorry."

"Well, that was pretty stupid, you know."

"What was?"

"Good Lord. When you've been having a problem to start with, and then when it's finally going well. Who'd stop to have me do something erotic in the middle of it?"

"Jess, it wasn't that. I was losing it."

"You were not."

"I was, I was."

"Well, not so it felt like to me. It couldn't have been better."

"Shit, shit, shit."

"All right, already. Just stop, will you? Talk about *post-coitum* sadness."

"Well this is hardly what the notion is all about."

"Still. Stop anyhow. It was lovely. And I was almost there. It will happen."

"When? Oh, piss on everything, it makes me feel so damned scruffy."

"Lucien, you'll know when I'm complaining."

"Come on. You were sore."

"Only the minute. When I misunderstood. Listen, I once had an affair that lasted a full summer. Almost every night. And I didn't come once."

"Thanks. That leaves me about three ahead. All from the first evening I was here."

"Actually two, as a matter of fact." Burst into laughter at that. "But who's counting?"

"Oh, you cunt."

"Poor worried Loosh. Get up and let's shower, I've got a zillion things to do in the morning."

Hunt a smoke when they're uncoupled, all goo's his maverick member. *Penis dejectus.* Or's he mean *foamento mori?*

"Nuts. Able was I ere I saw Elba. Or maybe I'm just getting old."

"Will you *please* quit? Lordy, you can be so impossibly Jewish every once in a while."

"Who? I'm Manichean, I think. Or Albigensian."

"And you're smashing in the sack also. Lucien, we'll get it back. So come on. I'll even do your hair again."

"The hell you will."

Attack him in there, however. Moment, does it take? All joyous with Jess afresh as under the spray he'll surrender, then grapple her to him with her cantaloupe bottoms full grasped. So thrilling too their flooded mouths predaceous.

Seesaw Sproosh. "God, I do love you. Even if I wasn't supposed to be here tonight to start with."

"Because of your sainthood? Or because this is no country for old men?"

"Nit. Or because of your mackerel-crowded pussy, how about? Anyway, maybe I'll write you an IOU. Innumerable orgasms."

"Only one problem."

"Tell me?"

Hand at his soapy scrotum, mirthful Jessie'll slyly squeeze.

"Just what have you got that you suspect is worth leaving as collateral?"

Been with his quail again, Springer's ransomed. First bearable morning in the three weeks.

Last through coffee's about the all, however. Who's the shitbreeches slipped in there betwixt, *sinopia* he over-painted on the sheets?

Adam Herschberger? Pythagorean Max finally get his theorem thrunked?

Marvelous. Slap-spang back where he was, so where's it heading this time?

Where Springer's heading most immediately's to a screening with Dana tonight. Insisted, thinks it a flick that might roust him off his butt himself.

Won't, hokey as most. Springer actually sat through anything's inspired him since *The Monty Stratton Story*?

Suggests a drink in the cab home. Place they'll pick'll be automatic.

Cornford in the rear? No workable opportunity for a gander.

And just how's the notion of an unorchestrated encounter grab him, Loosh done much weighty musing on the matter?

Cope with it if and/or. Awkward for Jess, senses, albumen all over her bodice. Though either way Dana'd come out ahead, more ease there, warmth's readier.

Enjoys being with her here now and again, tell the truth. Dane's admired, take time before people leave them to themselves.

Handsome new blouse also, finally enter his head to notice. "Is that Mexican?"

"This? Basque, I think."

"Anyhow, getting back. Never mind another screenplay. I just may have an idea for something else."

"A line of graffiti?"

"Edith Head gives good wardrobe. No, seriously."

"*Nu?*"

"The few evenings I've been with Jessica Cornford. She's told me quite a lot about herself, actually. Stuff I first thought I might use to revive that botch that went moribund on me last summer."

Drink while she's attending. Beautiful hands, forgets to remember.

"Suppose I took it from scratch again, using someone like Jessie instead of that older woman? But also a man like myself, say my age? And invented an affair?"

Eye him. "And?"

"Oh, well, who knows? Whatever must happen in those things. I guess I'd simply concoct some randy sex scenes for starters, see where it goes."

Unimpressed. Accepting the fictional premise as fictionally premised, at least? Sigh'd so seem.

"Lucien, *anything.* I've had so many extra office expenses lately I'm a wreck."

"Let me coddle it awhile. Maybe I'll pick Jessie's brain some more too. You want another one of those?"

"We'd better not. I've got hours of manuscript."

Wait at the door, one of her clients begging a last indulgence. Only now realizing why it struck him also, almost the identical blouse drying over Cornford's tub last night.

Oh, hallelujah. While there goeth Jess herself galumphing into the ladies' can.

Free the Butterfield Eight. Just as well collide with her right here, could.

Think twice next time at that. Springer truly want all his Basques in one exit?

Ten-fifteen, kids still toggled to the television.

"Hi. Did you see a good screening?"

"It was interesting, yes."

"It was awful."

Amusement for Doak there. "Mom likes them all, and Dad always says they smell."

"Because your mother has what are called crass, proletarian tastes. Your father's an artist."

"Your father's a grouch. Everything bores him. His brain is constipated."

"You definitely going to read now?"

"Lucien, will you look at that pile?"

"I guess I'll wander back over, you mind?"

"What happens if I do, plagues?"

Six minutes, means maybe twenty all told. Miljus at a table with a gaggle, Jess included? Other corner? Far wall?

Blood, frogs, vermin. Inquire of the good gray bard then, picked-over platter of ribs says he'll have been here throughout.

"*Paesano.* Tell me gently. She with a date?"

"You really are mortgaged. Did you make Dana jog home?"

"Life is earnest. Can we postpone the Hasidic commentary?"

"You just may re-enlist. The sort that wakes up the *shiksa* princess with a kiss. Dark, chiseled, might have been thirty. Nobody I ever saw before."

Beasts, murrain, boils, hail. "Thanks for nothing. That doesn't fit any of the half-dozen *already* on my list."

Wamble back out to the bar: who? Unless Wesley, she ever describe Wesley? Same one the other night also? Toss down his first new belt before Mike'll make change, poulticed liver be the way his novel'll end?

Or maundering through the *kaddish?* Rumpus of bandits in his belly, oh Jess, you screwing over there? *Thighness* of her, that luscious reliquary amidst. Who sloshing where Springer'd wallow his life away if he could?

Locusts, darkness, slaying of the firstborn. Slaying of the fairy prince, what he'd rather, Springer'll draw breath and dial.

He genuinely thinking about writing this? There possibly one dim reader in ninety couldn't forecast the next few lines? Hi, what are you up to? Oh, hi. Well, I'm talking with a friend.

"Hello?"

"Hi. What are you up to?"

"Oh, hi. Well, I'm talking with a friend."

Let my people go.

"Lucien, are you crazy or can you be drunk at ten o'clock in the morning? What do you mean, you told Dana it would be about us?"

"Made up, made up. Hell, are there any other girls your age she knows I've been spending time with? If I do write it and hadn't broached it that way it would be a lot more obvious."

"Oh, wow. Sometimes I do question your character."

"Blame yourself. You're the one with the rear end inspiring it all."

"Claptrap."

"You almost met her last night, by the way."

"Says when? How?"

"We had one quick one out front. Mostly I didn't know who you were with."

"Oh, he's the husband of a girl I once roomed with. They're in San Francisco. Lordy, I must have kept a smile pasted on through four hundred baby pictures."

Unbelievable, unbelievable. Tart do this *deliberately*, somehow?

"Did you say something?"

"Nothing, nothing. So what's your program for tonight?"

"I'm having dinner with a friend."

Springer once finally about to laugh here, maybe? Wail? Or pursue some trivial impulse for catharsis, better, like drop by at the Frick and splash peroxide on the El Grecos?

"Then again it's only semibusiness from the office. I'm certain I'll be home before ten, if you'd like to come over?"

Just calmly sob.

Semiboozeness, more the case, girl's vergingly squiffed. Deny it if he says, though practiced lush Loosh'll gauge it in her eyes.

"Hey, tell me. Did you save those poems I wrote?"

Lazing together at the tacky livingroom pillows, Jess'll contemplate tonnage on her file cabinets. "Somewhere, trust me. Why?"

"I didn't make copies. Use them in the book, possibly."

"Seriouser and seriouser, the man sounds. Do I still do Desdemona at the curtain?"

"*Quién sabe?*" Trace a knuckle along the seam of her jeans. "Jesus, stop gulping that stuff so fast."

"Silly. It's only wine."

"Don't be dumb."

"Not to worry tonight anyhow. I made a vow to get to sleep early, for a change."

Own heedless spoor as ever. She laundered linen in there, or's Springer's litter amid the other's still? Signatures of her screwings, latest communal art form.

"Actually I'd have more intricate problems. I mean besides inventing an ending."

"Such as?"

"The other men in your life, for one thing. Be ghosts. Names in passing."

"I've told you a lot about Jonathan Hundley, haven't I? And Max?"

"Tell me about Wesley."

"Why Wesley?"

"Be the protagonist's ultimate *bête noire*, I suspect."

Sense it in her now, even, flicker of sadness where she's pursed. Nudge Springer with desire, why're they here and not inside?

"How did you meet him? What's his last name, for that matter?"

"Sutcliff. He's an actor. He's a few months younger than I am."

Refilling there, sedimentary poison. "I was skiing. I'm better than the girls I'd gone with, and he and I fell in together. We had one of those exhilarating days that just happen, once in a while. I don't mean anything sexual, just the great runs, sensing challenges without having to say anything and then both of us outdoing ourselves, it was fantastic."

Swill down this one too, simp'll wish she could pawn her skull come morning.

"He had the use of someone's house, and later we talked until all hours. And he'd been so pleasant that I really believed him when he said he wouldn't make a pass if I stayed over."

Amused at herself momentarily, though wistfulness's the tenor still. "It was almost rape. I mean the first time. I was asleep, and then there he was in the room, and he literally did force me." Gazing into the lees, sigh's next. "After that he made love to me six more times in the one night."

Oremus. Titian live to be ninety-nine, they claim? Stand and offer Springer his subway seat, ah Christ.

"Is nympholepsy the word I want? We saw each other for eight months. I don't think we ever had to be in bed more than half a minute before my insides were oatmeal."

Bleak Jess, making them a pair. Shoulder's at his, rest of her's where, alas?

"Did I say he was married? Though he'd left her, eventually. But he just couldn't believe I wasn't being that way with other men also."

That a shudder? Up and stumbling, oh misery, she fleeing to weep now, even?

Wrong. Hand clapped to her mouth rather, crapper's where she's bolting. Now swell, just swell. Get there in time, at least?

Oh mistress mine, where're you retching?

On her hands and knees at the bowl, poor kid'll heave and heave. Nuts, poor everybody. Despairing Springer'll lift aside her sweated hair from behind.

Madonna of the shithouse floor. "Are you all right?"

"Oh, damn. Oh, fuck me."

Hauling her up when it's passed, ashen Jess. Did miss at first, spew's all over her.

"Here. Let me unbutton that."

"Wait. Never mind. Oh, Lord."

Into the shower with her clothes on instead, hang onto her elbow while she's negotiating.

"Don't slip, for Christ's sake."

"*Zut alors*. Llareggub spelled backwards."

Safely enough under, appears, he'll turn and flush. The throne she upchucked on, wipe gunk from the burnished seat as well.

"Lucien, let it be." Drenched, shirt's clinging where she'll struggle. "I'll do it later. The whole place must stink. Go, why don't you?"

"Finish, finish."

"Honestly. I'm fine now. I just feel squalid and stupid, is all."

Pants and panties next, meanwhile, vomity Venus emergent. Thy thighdom come.

"Lucien, do. I'm not going to screw. Not now."

"Jessie, just get your rump rinsed and on out, huh?"

Fold her into a towel when she does, look of skeptical remonstrance what he'll proffer?

Hands at her upper arms, sheepish wan smile what he'll finally get in return. "Oh, Lordy. I am woozy after all, I guess."

[*151*]

"Rummy."

Kissing her then? Peck's the intention. So whence the impulse to imbibe her mouth full fathom?

"Oh, Lucien. I must be foul."

"Go to bed, disgrace."

"You're nice, though. Disturbed, obviously, but nice."

Worst of it cleaned up? Drape the discarded wet gear at the faucets, Springer perhaps inclined to laugh at some of this now too?

Some, some. Retrieve his jacket, check back. All huddled and foetal, head's interred.

"You going to survive?"

"Ummm." Muffled. "I hope."

"I'll call you tomorrow."

"Ummm."

Anyway. Seven-times-a-night Wesley ever kiss her after she'd puked, that *macho* wiseass?

"Hello?"

"Lloyd George knew my father. Let's sing."

"Oh, God. Was I just awful?"

"What time did you get up?"

"Who says I am? Oww. Can you get a cheap prefrontal lobotomy in the neighborhood? Do they deliver?"

"It's almost eleven."

"I'll call in. They can have me as walking wounded in the afternoon, possibly."

Very timbre of her voice and Springer's longing for her anew. Still, two evenings out of three, smart to cool things a bit?

"Well, listen. Go back to sleep. I'll speak to you soon."

"All right. I'm busy tonight anyway."

Father knew Lloyd George. Had to slip that in, had to. Write his novel if only to fix her own damned wagon some way or other, just might.

Give the heroine bad breath?

"How's Jessie going to take it if you use her?"

"Less than scandalized. Anyway, she also knows it's the only game in town for me."

"You find out who young Launcelot was the other night, by the way?"

"Noncombatant, as it turned out. So tonight's a new blank and I'm ripe for Lethe all over again."

"Glut thy sorrow on a morning rose. Loosh, break it off."

Pike's risible, however, awaiting midnight *escargot*. Springer as ever'll merely guzzle obtusely on toward renal default.

"Anyhow, that's not the question for the minute. How the devil do you contrive a fictional structure for an experience when you're still in it up to your ass?"

"Test the options in reality, why don't you? Turn in your house keys."

"Prodigal. For art's sake?"

"Greater love. Or make yourself more of a *kvetch* with Cornford than you probably are already and get her to end it."

"*Cojones*. I guess I will."

"Which? Wait. Will what?"

"Jealousy. Lean on it until it snaps. If Springer can't have her nobody can, that sort of thing. Bread knife into the boscage."

"*Gevalt*. For this you need my garlanded consultation? Do I assume you'll call him something besides Springer?"

"Branca. Thomson. Mays."

"Why a bread knife?"

"Wolf's-bane make you happier? Lipp, the whole scheme's barely inchoate. One just happened to catch my eye in her kitchen last night."

Snails arriving, Pike'll chortle.

"Now what's funny?"

"You novelists, all that brooding. Too much *terra incognita* in the cortex. I'll probably open tomorrow's paper and turn to the obituaries before I even do the box scores."

Springer at all serious about any of that? Worth an
apathetic afternoon's once-upon-a-timing, at least?

Suppose, suppose, suppose. . . .

"Honey, I'm sorry. I love you, I always have. But I can't
help myself. We're using an inheritance Jessie just found
out about and leaving for Tehuantepec in ten or twelve
days."

"Lucien, I don't want to hear any more. Just get out of
here now, will you? Go. Please go."

"Hello?"
"Me. I'm in a pay booth. I just told her."
"Oh?"
"Christ, it was heartbreaking. Well, never mind. But
something I didn't think about. I can't stay there for the
rest of the time, obviously. I'll cart my junk out soon.
Meanwhile I'll ring your bell in a couple of minutes. Jess?"

"Well, listen. There's someone here. A friend."

"*Tonight? Tonight?* When you knew I'd be telling her?"
"Lucien, will you stop? I made it plain I'd be seeing
people almost every evening before we leave. Saying good-
bye."

"Saying good-bye *how?* And for Jesus' sake Max isn't
even one of the ones you were *supposed* to have been
screwing!"

"Lucien, it just happened. You know how close we've
been. I told him I was going and we got sentimental. Is
that so flagrant?"

"Oh, dear Lord, let me at least douche first then. I'm still dripping gallons from him."

"But it's only Adam Herschberger. And Miles Tinning on Thursday. And then Jonathan Hundley is driving down for the weekend. You must know there was no way I could leave without calling Jonathan Hundley, of all people."

"Lucien, how in heaven's name would you expect me to have an orgasm when we've been shrieking at each other like banshees since you walked in? Anyhow, I probably wouldn't have had one to start with. I was counting. I'd already come at least twenty-two times when Max was here."

"Oh, dear God above, Lucien, how could you? And with a *ski pole*? You kept stabbing her with a *ski pole*?"
"Dana, Dana, the girl tormented me so! Besides, tonight I couldn't find the bread knife."

"Hey, Dad, can I have about six rubber bands?"
"Blast it, Doak, how often do I have to explain that I'm *thinking*, out here?"

Alcohol. Insanity. Medullary compression of the gibbus. Add up to a drachma's worth of difference? Not about to write it anyway, ratcheted onto his rectum again. Still.

Not phoning again/still either, third day's this? Photo's on the desk when the apartment's quiet, however, bare-legged Jess. Where most recently, what tonight?

Same scortatory scumbag she balled last week, alack? Who?

Exultant novel. Seventy thousand words, middle-aged Abélard scratching around back of the sacristy where he lost something once that he can't even quite remember he ever owned.

And why in the name of Héloïse's uncle's pruning shears did Springer have to get her head filled with Wesley again, lugubrious inept *shmuck*?

Jess, Jess, we ever going to spinnaker into that simple single unfettered weekend even, wake once to sunlight and each other's arms?

These emerald Mahayana cogitations occurring on a Wednesday? Not yet noon's all he'll wager on, Springer's pouring his third. But why's he seem more scattered today than usual, inkling of something untoward in the air?

Arteriosclerosis of what he's parked on, about all's probable. Aware he's been shabby where old Maggie's concerned too, meanwhile, see if she's still hurting, should. Or's this just a second thought about unburdening some of his own sighs aplenty?

Ah, Oldring, swear you won't titter? My fault if you could bury the creature bottom-upward and use what'd protrude as a bicycle rack?

Mag turn frolicsome at news of an infestation of premature orgasms also? Becoming prematurer by the orgasm?

Compose a scene where she volunteers the aboriginal Old-ring orifice for practice till his stroke's come back, mayhap?

"Hello?"

"If you can keep yours hard when all about you are losing theirs and blaming it on you—"

"I beg your pardon?"

Oh, colorful. "Excuse me. Don't I have Oldring?"

"Lucien? Is that you?"

Voice he ought to know. "Who's that?"

"Karen Yeager."

"Karen, hey, not since forever." Mag's oldest and closest, good novelist, Springer'll go back decades with her himself. "On second thoughts skip Maggie. Something incomparably lascivious and corrupt finally, what do you say, Yeag?"

"Oh, Lucien, no jokes. Oh, dear, I guess I'd hoped you might somehow have already heard. We're only now making out a list of people to call."

"Karen?" Oh, now Christ. Oh, no. Springer been planning some kind of gingerbread autobiographical novel in which nothing worse than rueful ever happens? All eleven of his readers be positive this page's a misprint? "Yeag?"

"Lucien, Lucien, it's still so impossible. They were looking for something else altogether, and she just learned on Monday. Practically everything inside of her was rotted. And inoperable. It would have been a hideous few months, at best."

"Oh, Jesus heaven. Oh, Karen. And—?"

"Dear God, I'm so sorry. She took every pill in the house last evening. The maid found her about four hours ago."

Part Four

1

Brunelleschi and Donatello? Both young, digging methodically among ruined temples in Rome, measuring and scaling, and everyone assuming lost treasure the quest? Until Brunelleschi went back to Florence and put up the largest dome since antiquity?

Or the *Cappella Brancacci*, where poor absent-minded miraculous Masaccio who'd die by twenty-eight contrived those first frescos in which figures displace their own true depth, with solidity and mass not rendered by even Giotto? Where Michelangelo and Leonardo and Raphael would come in turn with copybooks to stand and stare?

And Piero? That unearthly, filtered, sourceless Tuscan light in Piero della Francesca, who'd himself pass on obscure and neglected and blind?

.... Spring? I do have four thousand dollars. From my grandmother, when I reached twenty-one last year. Take me there?

Mag, don't be drippy.

Why is it drippy? You're drawn to it so, and I've never gone even once. I'm dying to. And I'll bet we could stretch things for just ages also, if we were sensible. Or until you'd walk out on me for somebody's cow-bosomed Calabrian cousin with a mustache.

Are you even halfway serious? Mag? And with no more strings than we've had? Holy smokes, we could jump aboard some cheap freighter in a few weeks, probably.

Oh, Spring, let's. Let's!

Oh, Mag. Oh, not.

"It's all right, hon, I've already heard. I was trying to reach you, in fact."

"I had appointments away from the office. But it's just so unbelievable, nobody in town is talking about anything else. How did you find out?"

"I guess I forgot to say, she'd called last week. And mentioned that spine thing. So this morning I got the spectacular impulse to see how she was."

"Oh, Lord. You mean you dialed without knowing? Lucien, you must be in shock. I feel so badly myself."

"Dana, how wouldn't you? It's all these years for you now too, isn't it?"

"Don't you remember? Only three or four days after our first weekend together. You insisted there was one old girlfriend who had to approve."

"Oh, Christ. And then she didn't let either one of us get six words in through the whole lunch. And when I called later she wondered if you weren't too subdued for me. Oh, Dane, how can I be laughing and crying at the same time?"

"Sweetheart, if it were you instead of Maggie, don't you think she'd be repeating all those self-deprecating anecdotes about how cruel you were always supposed to have been? But, oh Lucien, wouldn't she also be grieving as deeply as anyone you'd ever known?"

.... Spring? Did I tell you about my vision?

Maggie, it's five o'fornicating clock in the morning.

Hold me and be quiet. Years and years from now, this is, when I'm horribly old. Forty, maybe. And I'm having this special dinner with T. S. Eliot.

Who'll just happen to be thoroughly deceased.

No he's not. He's all precarious and creaky, but he's sweet. In fact the reason for the dinner is to sort of anoint me, as the only poet since himself who's important. Maybe we'll let Ezra Pound be there too. And Robert Frost.

If they're humble and don't dribble their custard.

You won't think it's all that hilarious when we come out of the restaurant. And there you are panhandling on the corner. Except that you don't even recognize me anymore, because of how astonishingly glamorous I still look. And the way I'm glowing.

From sucking off all those ninety-year-olds?

That's my business. But maybe I'll just whisper to T. S. about you when we pass, too. How I was once doleful enough to let one scabious rat make me suffer so much.

Oh, nuncle, I should have realized. What this time?

What do you think, rat? Two nights ago, when you were supposed to be drinking with your French-Canadian friend. Kerouac?

Oh, hell. How did you find out?

Never mind how I found out.

You and that finky loyal coterie. Who saw me? Yeager? Just tell me, rat.

Mag, it wasn't anything anyhow. So I ran into a girl in a bar. As it turned out she bored me.

When? After you'd made love to her in eleven different positions and couldn't think of a twelfth?

Stop it. I didn't even keep her telephone number.

Oh, now isn't that ameliorating. Did you take a shower also, hopefully? Staggering in here shitfaced at four o'clock and being slimy all over me? God.

I wasn't that drunk. As a matter of fact I've got a pretty vivid recollection of having said I loved you.

Oh, bountiful. All putrid with somebody else's reek and he's finally guilty enough to declaim something tender. For the first time in the three separate times that we've lived together. Jesus, I'm cursed. Oh, you bastard. So will you at least bite your tongue and say it again? Now? Oh, damn you, Spring. Even though I know you're trapped, will you?

Oh, Oldring, did I? Please?

"Hello. Is this Lucien Springer?"

"Speaking."

"Hi. It's Phoebe Cissell. From the magazine with Jessica."

"Oh, sure. How are you? What's up?"

"Well, I'm at the office. I was just talking to Jessie on one of our Washington trunks."

"Hell. When did they disappear her down there?"

"Only this morning, a kind of rush fill-in for someone else. Until early next week, I gather. In any case, what she asked me to call about was Maggie Oldring. Golly, I wasn't aware you were close. I'm terribly sorry."

"Thank you."

"But that's being clumsy, isn't it? I mean since obviously it's what Jessie wanted said herself. That she was shocked and hopes you're not too upset."

"I appreciate it."

"Oh. And also that she sends love."

"Have you got a more direct quote on that last, maybe? Sends it how? Like on a postcard from cousin Blanche in Tijuana?"

"Oh, literally that, sort of. Though judging from the two minutes I saw you with each other I don't guess I was completely guyed, you should pardon the presumption?"

"But all she actually said was would you tell him love too, please?"

"Pin me down. It was, yes."

"Ah, well. Anyway, thanks again, Phoebe. Take care."

"You also. *Ciao.*"

Ah, Jess. Ah, Mag. Ah, life.

. . . . Be truthful, sot. How many times can you try before it becomes satire? Or plain farce?

Tell me about him.

His name is Arnold Danforth. Don't grimace, but he's in corporate finance. I could subsidize any twenty of your degenerate saloon chums out of the egg money, if I do.

Your age?

Yours, really. Divorced. Does it make sense to say that he means well, Spring? About everything? Lord above, all three of the others were such brackish disasters. What do you and Dana know that nobody else seems to? Is it fifteen years?

Closer to seventeen.

Gad. Anyhow, stay here like this awhile longer, can you? I am sort of disenthralled and full of lamentations these days. Or hadn't you surmised?

Voices singing out of empty cisterns and exhausted wells?

Or dry sterile thunder without rain, does he say? Still, I do somehow manage to keep up the charade for the rabble, don't I?

And still she cried, and still the world pursues.

Spring, Spring, Spring. Or is it just that I'm so saggy-assed weary of prancing through life fucking strangers?

"Are you still awake?"

"Yes."

"I'm grateful you stayed home. Gosh, it just becomes more and more heartbreaking. What kind of a marriage was this last one, did you ever hear?"

"Looked serviceable the once or twice we met him. Why?"

"Oh, you know the talk. Every third week, some alleged new Maggie escapade. It does seem true that she was drunk at her readings almost everywhere lately."

"Hell, Dane, people thrive on that *dreck*. For that matter there's probably no little scatological local bullshit about me and Jessica Cornford by now, too."

"What is that supposed to mean, exactly? Why would there be?"

"Oh, well, even if I no more than run into her over there. Or then walk her home."

"That's charming."

"Now since when do you give a damn about that sort of moronism? Anyway, there's something rather more dolorous I've been lying here with."

"Lucien, what?"

"Mag. When she called last week. She was on her way to a doctor down here and she asked me to sit with her. I dredged up some counterfeit excuse."

"Oh, dear, how could you? Why?"

"You know how defrocked and impotent I've been feeling. She caught me on an afternoon when I was practically ready to drink eisel."

"Good Lord."

"Dana, don't you think I've been miserable about it all day?"

"I should certainly hope so."

"Though it obviously sounds a lot more seamy now. Who had any notion, for Jesus' sake?"

"Lucien, but still."

"I suspect I also didn't go because of Arnold, partly."

"What would Arnold have to do with it?"

"Who knows how he'd have taken it if she told him she'd called me?"

"What are you talking about? Why shouldn't he have been delighted that she had an old friend in the neighborhood?"

"Come on, he must be aware I used to live with her."

"My God, you are sick. I don't think there's anybody else in this world who looks at things the way you do."

"More people do than don't."

"No one I know does. Dear heaven, Lucien. I honestly sometimes wonder."

"Oh, damn it. Damn it."

"Now what?"

"The whole mournful fucking business. All the jeremiads, whatever. What difference does any of it make?"

"Some. Somehow it does. You should have gone."

"Oh, Christ, I know. Oh, Dane, I do feel so shitty. Hold me for a while?"

"Lucien, Lucien. Are you crying again?"

"It just keeps coming back. All of a sudden she seems so important in my life."

"Honey, as I said, she cared about you. Oh, dear."

"What?"

"Now I'm the one sobbing and laughing at once. I'm sorry. But after you solve that, can you also tell me why in heaven's name I'm still in love with you myself?"

7

Why, indeed? Springer's destiny just pure and simple serendipitous?

Or because he's slithered into total deviousness so winsomely now too, perfidious lying bastard? Cauterize any gossip again before any does get back to her.

Or because his head's scarce so twisted as she believes either, bloody well more husbands than Arnold having fair cause to view him aslant?

Or because it's fact that he never did own quite enough love for Maggie, for all the true salt of loss? Give him three minutes for these latest tears to cease, be rapaciously embracing new visions of Jessica Cornford's sugarplum backside again also.

Just plain lucky Loosh at that, must be. To know the darling is to adore him.

"Brother, it's left me wasted. What an indelibly handsome piece of talent. I assume you saw the obituary?"

"How not?"

"I'll pass up any tarnished gag I might have intended about looking for Cornford's. Meanwhile it should only happen to me."

"Which? Inoperable cancer, or the bottle and a half of Seconal?"

"Thanks. I meant all that space. Do you know what time things are scheduled for tomorrow, by the way?"

"Hey, Lipp. Hey, Loosh. You guys hear about the tragedy in Warsaw? The national library burning to the ground? With both books destroyed?"

"Piss off, Lester."

"Lester, we're talking about a funeral."

"Wait. And one of the books hadn't even been colored yet?"

Suckle fools and chronicle small vodka. Life does go on.

Avicenna read Aristotle's *Metaphysics* forty times. Mozart was buried in an unmarked grave. Aeschylus fought at Marathon and Salamis and then died when an eagle dropped a turtle on his head. Thomas Lovell Beddoes once tried to set fire to the Drury Lane Theater with a five-pound note. Alexander razed Thebes but left untouched the house that had been Pindar's. St. Isadora in an urgency to be contemptible subsisted upon swill from the floor of a monastery kitchen. Jules Pascin scrawled a farewell to his mistress in blood after opening his wrists. Fichte, Schelling, and Hegel taught at Jena at the same time. Beethoven contracted his ninth symphony to two separate publishers. Christy Mathewson died of tuberculosis at Saranac Lake. Maupassant, insane, ate his own excrement. The Ghent altarpiece had already existed for fifty years before Columbus. François Villon disappears from history at thirty-two, what rest unknown. Rembrandt's possessions were auctioned at bankruptcy in the same town and in the same month that only blocks away Spinoza was excommunicated. The life of man in a state of nature is solitary, poor, nasty, brutish, and short. Voltaire wrote *Candide* in three days, Erasmus wrote *The Praise of Folly* in seven. The grave's a fine and private place, but none, Springer thinks, do there embrace. Men have died from time to time, and worms have eaten them, but not for love. Springer hast committed fornication, but that was in another country, and besides, the wench is dead.

Once too, a beautiful lemon-haired poet told him of a child's terrible fantasy in which flowers turned demons to pursue her, but probably she fibbed, because never later did she write it down.

And now Springer's at her final flowered ceremony, and

some fragile antic wingèd thing's what's in his mind, wheeling tremulous but ah, so gaudy against the day! Wild thing! So how then's this she, now wracked and broken on the strand?

And his youth gone with her now also? The richest of it, youth's last fond remembered hungers and the raging hopes? From that secret warm bright corner of his heart that's been forever Mag? Oh, damn you, girl, this swift? This soon?

For who then can ever lead him back, or name him that place where all the dreams went dark?

Part Five

Just as well Cornford's away, Springer's en route from grimmer to grimmest. Onto something now that he'd only been toying with before. Get to work soon or he'll sink through the carpeting altogether.

Weekend's debilitating in either case. Certain his miscarried old manuscript's irreclaimable. So just where's his Jessie tale wind up with that scheme for killing her such incunabular rubbish?

Pall from the funeral naturally persisting too, poems stacked at the corner of his desk. Snip a portrait from one of the dust jackets finally, tack it beyond.

Mag near his window, Jess misty in the lower drawer. He and she decamp for Mexico after all, write it that way? All idyll and balmy juvenescence?

Dreamy *malheurs* in Mag's photo'll promptly enough contravene that twaddle. Plus words from Karen Yeager still knotting him as well, "Oh, Lucien, you'll never know how often she talked about you, even after all these years." Novelist, ostensibly? Go construe life first.

Then again, absent himself from infelicity awhile and try to do Mag, maybe? Unpawn the memories and redeem old guilts? We have heard the chimes at midnight, Mistress Oldring?

Or's all this the bleakest joke yet? John-a-dreams here, disengage his desert boots from the typewriter and then what? Contemplate verdigris on the keys.

Same for his leucorrheal brain. Examine it like a vagina and moths'd blink out.

Back betimes, Cissell say? Won't pick up over there until Wednesday.

"Hey, Jess. Hi. When did you get in?"

"Oh, a couple of days ago, in fact. Hi."

So there go Springer's skittery viscera as ever, anything altered? What's the mattress-bottomed wretch been up to?

"I did try you the other afternoon, Lucien, but I never really know when it's all right to call. Tell me about the funeral. How do you feel?"

"Oh, the obvious, pretty much. Bum stretch."

"It's all anyone seems to be talking about still. Glory, and now I keep realizing how sorry I am I didn't let you introduce me."

"I am too. We'll talk. You loose tonight."

"I'm seeing a friend. In fact it's as if I can't find a minute for myself, lately. Ever since Ohio."

Tremendous, Springer's ecstasied. Still drained from Mag, now this one'll suck up the last few drams.

"Though I'm having dinner with Norma Miljus tomorrow. At guess where, if you'd like a drink or two afterwards? Someone else is stopping by also, but I don't think for very long."

Forsooth. Or'd seven minutes one week from Whitsun be more convenient?

"Oh, well, good. I'll catch you then."

Party of the second part's grandly ambiguous too, nary a pronoun betokening. Dissect her own whoreson brain one day instead of his, what he ought. There some gleeful homunculus hopping around in there, keeps semaphoring fuck Springer up?

Ten-ish when he'll show, milky old Miljus this early
exiting? Sly smirk for him where he'll hold the door as
they converge.

"So, Milj?"

"How you doing, kiddo? Your, um, pardon me, friend,
is out yonder."

"Now which friend would that be?"

"Fuck not about with the house sibyl, lad. Matter of
fact the oracle reads run don't walk."

"Oh, Christ."

Solving that unspoke pronoun's gender, 'sblood, unsur-
prised Springer'll wearily wince and wave her off.

So there's Cornford seemingly solo rather, all gladness and
smile. Or not quite, redundant drink adjacent, flight bag
below that seat. Matter? Have him bubbly at the beckoning.

"Damn. It is a fact."

"Lucien, hello. What is?"

"You're even attractive without the vomit."

Response'll peal. "Oh, stinker!"

Dozen seconds all he's granted, however, and then just
ask him what odds he'd have given. Seafaringly handsome,
rotter'll edge him by at least fifteen years as well.

"Donald. Did you find it?"

"Interesting graffiti. What does it mean that Lippman
Pike gives better wardrobe?"

"Sit again. Donald Rosen, Lucien Springer."

"My pleasure."

"Hello."

Tiresias was the first seer sucker. So who's this one, for
Beelzebub's sake? Wasn't Springer pretty damned sure he
had the list?

"Donald was the one good writing instructor I had as
an undergraduate. He also got me my first job."

Salaam aleikum. Likewise her first graduate boff? Mooning at her like a schnauzer, when'd they see each other last?

Bobby Franks was a snot. Bastard aware Springer's her date? Waitress just disappearing when he'll glance in that direction.

"Get you another beer, Jessie? One of whatever, Don?"

Deign less than a gesture over there, still rapt. "No more for me. I'm afraid I do have to make that drive, Jess."

Off a cantilever. Cornford caught up in turn, eyes even watery? Or's she just too heavy into the night's potion again?

Rosen finally back on his feet at least, so now he'll letch over her hand for a bit. "It was great. I will give you that call."

"Do. I wish it had been longer."

Ultimately a nod for Springer. "Fine meeting you."

Infielderish gait too then, predictably, Springer himself had any exercise since the Truman administration? Watch Jess watch him away.

"Isn't he nice? He goes to Montauk. They start fishing practically before the sun comes up, if you can imagine?"

"I told you all about that. If Ahab knew, he'd have had Queequeg after your *tush* instead."

Melt to her at the appreciative laugh, ah Jesus, Springer give a fart about some sentimental years-ago screw? Anything he knows himself except he's the one with her again? Waitress nearby now also. "You want some more of that, Jess?"

"Actually I seem to have tubs of wine at home. Shall we, rather?"

Ahab, you hab, Springer hab. Oh, true, right here beside's where the great whale ariseth.

Moby Buttocks. While so much for thee indeed, young Rosen, Springer's felicitations to the polliwogs and the sardines.

"Perfume of embraces all him assailed. With hungered flesh obscurely, he mutely craved to adore."

"You're in a mood?"

"The working class can kiss my ass. I've got the foreman's job at last."

"Was the first one Joyce? I think there's beer, by the way. If you don't want the Chianti?"

Finding it. Though well nigh asphyxiated at the quest. "Ods bodkins, woman, what venomous kind of cheese is that?"

"Do I have cheese? I don't. It must just be something left over."

"Horse, horse. From the tenant before last?"

Join her amidst the livingroom detritus, Springer'll accommodate himself with his head at her hip. Less sauced than he'd thought, though she's seeming remote. Or'd mention of Mag while they strolled disturb her?

"You and he have a whatchamacallit, speaking of by the ways?"

"Donald? Not very long, yes."

"*Qué pasó?*"

"He's footloose, essentially. We just drifted."

"Knew he didn't seem particularly astute."

Draw her down then, so commodious as always their coupling. Yet curious too, ache's so often an abstraction, possible he sometimes forgets how simple a thing he's aching for?

Mr. Leopold Bloom ate with relish the inner organs of beasts and fowls. *Chacun à son goût*, Mr. Lucien Springer'll pucker at unbuttoned breasts and think venereal. Feasts and bowels. Then slip her skirt away as well, where kneeling he'll nuzzle linted navel.

"Jess, Jess, Jess."

No answer when he'll lie again soft stroking, Jess near naked and himself most clothed. Write these moments and not induce boredom, eternal fugitive *sameness* of such? How many times the rose leaves die of grieving in a single book?

Or'll a bladder digression brighten his prose? Discarding his shirt en route, why's Jessie fallen so silent?

"Hey, Jess. It just strikes me I've never recited you my favorite poem. From his Clongowes period, according to recent scholarship. Can you hear? Little boy kneels at foot of the bed, little hand sturdy 'neath little blond head. Drip, drip, into the tank, Christopher Robin is taking his wank."

Distracted still despite. At the bed when he'll emerge, however, all inadvertent pelvis her posture. Thigh will be done. With relish. Merge Cunard Lines and Aer Lingus and what do they call the conglomerate?

"Lucien, wait."

Leg and three-quarters out of his pants. "Ummm?"

"I don't want to make love with you tonight."

And what is home without Plumtree's Potted Meat? Attentive, some reason he might just deduce on his own? Various, all lately premature. But now heck.

"Jess? What's all that about?"

"Oh, damn. Because I've been screwing all week, is why."

Oh, no. Oh, Christ, stomachless, help. Empedocles leave his sandals behind when he vaulted? See Springer trail trousers and sag.

"Oh, well, I hardly mean all week, obviously. When I got back, the first few days."

While Pico della Mirandola read twenty-two languages. And was dead at thirty-one, he skip the hard parts?

"Tell me who."

"Lucien, I was. What difference does it make?"

"Was it the same one from last time?"

Consider him in puzzlement.

"After Ohio. That first week, when I didn't call."

"Oh. No. That was Miles Tinning, I think."

"Now Jesus. You *think*?"

"Well, I saw him recently. Yes, that would be when."

"And this was somebody else?"

"Yes. Lucien, I'm not going to tell you. I've said, I've got to be discreet about people."

Cold of interstellar space, Springer'll chew lip and straggle off for their drinks. That one tonight, he misinterpret their not having seen each other? She do that to him, sit him down with the mother?

Supine now, arm across her eyes. So what need to let himself in for any of it, someone apprise him? Ask, one glance even now and intestinal trauma'll elucidate.

One of the languishing household non-fucks suddenly sprout, Herschberger or Max?

"Was it nobody new, at least?"

"Lucien, it was nobody new. Can you stop? And will you do me a favor, please? Just lie here with me?"

Or even that, then? Yes, misery grisery, let Jess snuggle while Springer'll settle, his pun's intentional. Enfold that plundered mellifluent eloquence of her, gold doubloon to the hand first fondles the great pink posterior.

Secondbest bedness. Yet the grievance already half out of mind from this alone, book be these hundred antiphonal mermaid singings after all?

So why's Cornford shivering the meantime, cheeks of a sudden runneled?

"Jess?"

"Oh, Lordy, I'm so fucked up. Just hold me?"

"Oh, Jess."

And all of his own spurious whining, ah Christ. She even see Wesley perhaps, that keenest hurt for her rekindled? Or just the so many others and none right?

"Jess, listen. I keep intruding, and I know there's so little for you in return. If part of it is my fault, I'm sorry."

"It's not, Lucien."

Or only life then? Only. Taste tears at her nearer cheek, what longing whetted that Springer cannot ever answer for her but would, but would?

"Poor old horse."

"Will you do something else for me too?"

"You know I will."

"Stay here until I fall asleep? And after, for a while? Like this?"

"Of course."

Be moments at best in any case, ever precipitous her drowsings. Huddled to him, sad lovely Jess, more lonely and less strong than blindered Springer'd seen, whatever.

Not yet twelve, give her hours even, God-a-mercy. While with hungered flesh obscurely, mutely craving to adore.

Dominus vobiscum. And thereafter, oh spurned though succoring swain?

Drip, drip, into the sack, Springer another be taking his whack?

Time to creep into the wainscotting again? Or's this all he ever seems to be deliberating?

Shortchanged old Jess. Miscreant Springer visualizing her fallopian-deep in undying romance, and what's Cornford apparently ponder but melancholy near misses and impermanence?

Drag her sutured *tuchas* off to Boston with the perennial Jonathan, sometimes wishes, knocked up forthwith and soonly bellying. Repeal Springer's mucusy *mishegas* thataway?

Requiescat. So meanwhile who's this latest, ah damn?

"Hello?"

"Good morning."

"Lucien, Lucien. Will you tell me why I drink so much?"

"You weren't bad."

"I'm sorry if I acted some splendid kind of bitch?"

"Hell, Jess, I'm the one. What do I have for you?"

"That's sort of a proleptic question, isn't it?"

Not quite bloodied by the summary accord? Or's he merely for the moment feeling meliorative?

"Anyway, let me change the subject. Melodramatic news."

"You set fire to your truss?"

"Claybrains. I just walked back in this instant. With two reams of copy paper and some ribbons."

"Hey! Are you really going to get started?"

"Now all I need are some words."

"Stop. In fact you're probably more darned sesquipedalian than's good for you. But listen, all kinds of luck. I mean that."

"I'll call you."

"Do."

Articulate Loosh? Verbally vested and etymologically equipped?

So which fucking fucker's she fucking?

Now is the rime oops time for all ogog men to fome
to the aid of their artpy
   The quick brown fxo jumped over the lazy dog's back
   How like a winter hath my absence been from
   the day of her deatj was a
   The brick frown quox upmed jover the bazy log's dack
pissssssssshittttttt   eeeeeejackufuckinglation!!
   Call me Springer /// howdy do, i am her mgsty's dg
at Kew
   give me a cup of sack, rogue, is there no virtue extant
???

   bruno hauptmann was innocent (gisned) the lndbrg baby
                        yet once more o ye laurels
HORace Ovid Catullus Lucretius Kurtissimus Vonnegutus
asdfghjkl;¢ A GREAT HORROR AND DARKness fell
upon Christian 1=234567890-¾+"#$%—&'*!! obscenity
in the milk of thy
   *Ave Caesar, morituri te salutamus. Facilis descensus
Averni.* Return with yr shield or on it. Achilles absent was
Achilles still. God is necessary and so must exist. Job en-
dured everything until his friends came to comfort him
then he GREW IMPATIENT if you think L. Springer
said that it was S. Kierkegaard now is the Domenikos Theo-
tocopoulos Cezapples *iacta alea est*
   st jude patron st of fuckedup fuckups where art thou
   o maggie o maggie o maggie O
   magjessdane   comejesscome
   catamenia promulgates pederasty but if you boiled a
Syriac bible wld you get an inspissating Peshitta ??
   ARE the commentators on HAMLET Really mad or
only pretending to be ??

goldgotha
jug jug   twit twit   shantih
yes i will yes
FURTHERMORE ?

Piddle through the weekend thus, skull's vermiculated. Dana know some kindly editor might issue a slim, blank-paged tome as a courtesy, look upon Springer's works ye mighty and despair?

"Lucien, good heavens, think how much fallow time there's been. As long as you're finally sitting there."

"I guess. Partly it's that Maggie keeps butting in too, as if it's her I ought to write about. But that reminds me. You care if I see Jessica tonight?"

That eyebrow a reflex by now? Or's Springer sensing shaded areas?

"Dane? She was going to do some work first, and I said I'd dial again from the saloon. I don't have to, if you're unhappy about it?"

"Lucien, I don't mind if you see her. Especially if it might help you get started."

"Well I wish you wouldn't look so solemn?"

"Oh, it's probably just money again, as usual. It's already past time to be thinking about camp. That's fifteen hundred dollars for each of them."

"Onerous Jesus. You going to have it?"

"I'll just have to."

"Listen, I will get into something. And you know how hard I work once I'm at it."

"You're asking a major reclamation of memory."

"*Shnook.* But something genital and quick this time, too." Grin when he'll buss her brow. "As soon as I stumble onto what it's conceivably all about."

Does deplore leaving her in depression, though. Takes that fine paranoid edge off his own.

"Hi. What time is it?"

"Ten-forty-five, going on."

"Well, listen. Why don't you give me one more hour? To finish typing what I'm at now?"

Three vodkas and a passing sulk's worth. What's she been into since Thursday, who's that last shitkicker she unhooped for?

Hallelujah, gloom moderately alleviated when she'll greet him flush out of the shower and still dropleted? Knotted stringy red bath towel all betwixt Oliver and the oatmeal, see Springer *kvell* at the simulated conjugality.

Scrubbing her hair dry also, ah sweet armpittedness of life. "Come in. All of a sudden I felt cruddy. But hey, guess what?"

"Macwomb was from his mother's duff untimely ripp'd. What?"

"I'm back exactly where I was. All those first chapters, completely revised."

"Jess, beautiful. You going to try them on your agent?"

"Am I not? Oh, golly, wouldn't it be something if he thinks they're good enough to get me an advance?"

Springer's unstopping new wine. Then decanting same into a tin kitchen measuring cup, wouldn't it be something if she'd rinse an annual glass?

"But meanwhile what about you?"

"Don't ask. Page number minus-fifty and suppurating."

"That's silly. You've just forgotten what an ordeal it always is."

"Tell me, wetnose."

Trailing her to the couch. Oblivious old fleshly Jessly, beguile him to near infarction simply in tucking up her legs. Queasy queer crimping in his gut though too? Is. How many more bollixed-up uptuckings of his own sort here before he'll confront quarantine instead?

"Are you all right, by the way?"

"How, Lucien?"

"The other night."

"Oh, Lordy. I do revel in self-perpetuating bullshit, sometimes."

"Hell."

"Seriously, though. Where are you really?"

"I meant it, no fix on anything. I seem to keep focusing on Maggie, one idea more mawkish than the next. Or on somebody like myself being touched by her, say, except I haven't a clue about who I want myself to be, what voice I'm after. Get back to raunchy Jess Cornford as intended, I suspect."

"I told you you're welcome. All the slatternly details."

"One I need elaboration on."

"Which?"

"Since the Washington trip. Who you screwed."

"Lucien, I said I won't say."

"What's his first name, at least?"

"Gee, it was so earthshaking I forgot to ask."

"Cunt." Bend to peck her shoulder at that, however, lost instanter to the cool damp briny sweetness that's Jess. "Now, balls."

"My pleasure. Balls what?"

"How the devil can I do a book with this on every eighth page also? Three days of sniveling, then one touch and I couldn't care if you were gangbanged. By choice. How many of your maternal great aunts did they string up at Salem?"

"Fire burn and cauldron bubble. Will you let me put a different sort of hex on you, then?"

"Such as?"

"My manuscript. I honestly did just finish. I think it's scads better, Lucien, but I am sort of scared shitless. Is this beastly of me tonight? Would you?"

Lechery's labor lost. Watch her scamper after it once he'll gesture, unwitting flash of friendly neighborhood fanny in return for his largesse, even.

Lothario Loosh. Doubtless mop her floors and sing next too, cross the vixen's mind to ask.

"For Christ's sake, wake up."

"Gnnh?"

"Simpleton."

Bottom billowing for fair now, towel unrigged in there and an opened paperback snatch-unto that he'll dislodge. *Go Down, Moses?* "Jessie, it's magnificent."

"Hey, I'm sorry. Are you finished?"

"Will you listen? I almost can't believe it's the same novel."

"Now come on."

"I swear, the whole thing's so much more intensely realized I don't know where to start. Even characters who were ciphers I'd forgotten altogether. But it's the girl, Susanna. All those new perspectives you've thrown her into and she practically bounces off the page."

"It's you I owe for that."

"Balderdash."

"No. You drink so much you probably don't remember. But my uncertainty with point of view is what you were shrewdest about."

"Screw. So meantime who put together that prose? Some of it is so resonant it vibrates. In fact I'll tell you something."

"Oh, Lucien. What?"

"After Mag's funeral, her editor mentioned that someone is already talking about a biography. But now I'm going to make damned sure a few dozen of my least discreet friends know about the two of us, also. I plan to surface one day as the most envied bedroom footnote in American literature."

"Nerd. Oh, but I am excited. No matter how outrageously you're exaggerating."

"Jess, I'm not. I may really get off my own ass now out of envy alone."

"Glory, I hope so. Is your watch right, by the way?"

"Oh, hell. How can it have gotten this late?" Kissing her. "You're foul. You're also a blinking genius. Quit that magazine."

Contented Jessica, breasts buoying where she'll complacently stretch, fistful of Springer's innards the sight'll clutch.

"Go. Oh, Lucien, I do appreciate it."

Footnote: Data *re* sexual aspects of the Springer–Cornford liaison remain inconclusive, though it is Mr. Springer's considered opinion that on certain obscure occasions they possibly fucked.

May that as it be. Springer's meant every word, creature'll have him jaunty the six blocks.

Means it about attacking that recalcitrant machine of his
own now too, by God. Garrote the bloody thing. Tomorrow, psalms to Jessica.

So what exactly's this, meanwhile? House full of an
unnatural lurking quiet, why's it seem almost palpable?
Amy or Doak contrive some mischief at his desk? Oh
Jesus, dagger before him rather:

It's 4:05. Where WERE you?

Castrated Pollux, not six minutes since. Obviously still
awake and extrapolating in there, means.

"Dana? Can I turn on a light?"

"Don't."

"Now hell, I'm sorry. I simply got stuck. I didn't go
over until midnight, and then she'd just tonight finished
revising that whole section of her manuscript I'd seen."

No answer, though in faintest window light he'll sense
her sitting. Delighted also at the ironic innocent veracity
of his tale, is he?

"It turned out to be almost twice as long, this time. And
I could hardly run off without talking to her about it
afterwards."

Still *nada*, Springer'll shed clothing opposite. "Come on,
Dane. Anyway, it's sheer chance that you woke up.
There're times I've closed the saloon at this hour, too."

"I didn't wake up. I hadn't been asleep."

"Oh, well. But still."

"All right, Lucien."

"Is that supposed to sound as if you don't believe me?"

"I didn't say that."

"And it is her first try at fiction."

"You've told me."

Ah, Christ. Knew she was upset when he went out, forget Ducky Medwick's lifetime batting average after ten seconds with Jess. She shuddering there, no less?

"Oh, Dane. Are you trying to make me start feeling swinish, now?"

"Lucien, I'm not."

"What is it, then?"

"I don't know."

"What we were talking about before?"

"I just seem to work so hard. And it keeps going out so fast."

"Sweetheart, I promised you. I will get started."

"Oh, maybe it's still Maggie also, how sudden it was. It seems to hover and hover."

"I know. But now damn, it is late. In fact you're not leaving for that bunghole office before noon."

"Lucien, I have morning appointments."

Easing downward at least, Springer'll lean to kiss her.

"Hon, I am sorry. It was just a fluke. Do feel better, please?"

"Yes."

Injunbite anew then finally? Out, damned spot? Old mandrake dogsbody sleepmurderer Loosh?

And yet, and yet, and yet. Can any of it be so nefarious all in all, finally? Is it? After all their seachanged, wayworn years, his and Dane's, near a lifetime's moiety, Springer someway truly holding her any less dear for moment's want of Jessie too?

"Dane? I do love you, just incidentally."

"I know you do, Lucien."

Sighing therewith. As in long-battened domesticity they nestle buttocks to bum, the latter word being safely taken, he trusts, in at least one other of its several purports.

Oldring Oldring Oldring Oldring, summoned monthly by the lustered moon'd she say?

While Jessica Cornford has bourbon hair and hyacinth eyes and an opulent Orphic ass.

And Springer's imperishable hero in turn'll be precisely what, maybe? Ossified ovarian opportunist?

Onomatopoetic obfuscations of onanism. Here he is, an old man in a dry month and never ever even saw his prepuce, please send alms.

"Hello?"

"Help!"

"Shit, Lucien, I was sleeping."

"Hell. I'll call you back."

"Oh, never mind, it's time anyway. What's wrong?"

"What's not? Three days, and my one aesthetic achievement is tincturing each morning's first few drinks with orange juice."

"Lucien, don't be asinine. How long did your last book take?"

"Hmmm. Three years?"

"*Nu*, rummy? Meantime listen, I should have called to say thank you again. I never touched the floor all that next morning."

"So when am I going to see you? Now I'm the one running scared."

"These few days are impossible, I'm afraid."

Leonardo da Vinci was lefthanded. Like Warren Spahn?

"Jonathan Hundley is coming down."

Ah, well, holds off the rest of the bohunks too, at least. "He staying long?"

"Tomorrow and Friday he has business. But then we may do his Pennsylvania place if the weekend is nice."

Jess and Dane and pray for rain. "Cornford, Cornford. Desert me in my time of trial."

"Lucien, stop moaning. Just sit down and scribble any old opening to goose yourself. Worry about making sense later."

"Thanks."

Frowzy snotnosed young slut with her thirty thousand words on paper.

It was the best of times, it was the worst of times. Well, Prince, Genoa and Lucca are now no more than private estates of the Bonaparte family. Now is the winter of our discontent. In my younger and more vulnerable years my father gave me some advice that I've been turning over in my mind ever since. Robert Cohn was once middleweight boxing champion of Princeton. Sing, goddess, the wrath of Achilles, Peleus' son. Two mountain chains traverse the republic roughly from north to south. She waited, Kate Croy. Alice was beginning to get very tired of sitting by her sister on the bank, and of having nothing to do. For a long time I used to go to bed early. The *Nellie*, a cruising yawl, swung to her anchor. Of man's first disobedience. According to the Persians best informed in history, the Phoenicians began the quarrel. Even Camilla had enjoyed masquerades. Mother died today. From beyond the screen of bushes which surrounded the spring, Popeye watched the man drinking. The cold passed reluctantly from the earth. I don't know how you found me, but since you're here you might as well come in and sit down. Who's there? Nay, answer me. Stand, and unfold yourself. Whan that Aprille with his shoures soote. The first hexagram is made up of six unbroken lines. There was a man and a dog too this time. Hale knew they meant to murder him before he had been in Brighton three hours. We are talking now of summer evenings in Knoxville, Tennessee. The seat on which Dobbs was sitting was a thoroughly bad one. Arms, and the man I sing. Gil and I crossed the eastern divide about two by the sun. Sitting beside the road, watching the wagon mount the hill toward her, Lena thinks, I have come from Alabama, a fur piece. None of them knew the color of the sky. O for a Muse of fire. *Nel mezzo del cammin di nostra vita.* In the beginning God created the heaven and the earth.

Once upon a time?

Springer start seeing Cornford before the last time he balled Maggie? No, obviously, only extramural jeans he's been into since Jessie're Jessie's.

But how's he write it in the real chronology if that puts Oldring up front? She likely to dye the whole pot inky for him?

Or'd he at least have a hard-on for Jess before that? Did, wasn't their first night already set when he ran into Mag on Eighth Street?

This girl, this horsy Jess Cornford with the Winslow Homer blouses and the sexy, cartilaginous neck, lead someplace?

Springer given any thought to fictional names for these people either, meanwhile? *Cojones*, later, least of his worries.

Lurking anent the ladies' latrine? Eye out for this wench who's just ducked inside, this clodhopper Cessica Jornford?

He commencing to hear a tone now in any case? Close enough to the crotch? Or's he still not sure just who's Loosh?

Shlemiel of shreds and patches. Obliquitous *borracho* jackanapes, *aussi*. Yet mayn't the straggler be pilgrim of sorts still, however oft by his pecker untracked?

Indeed, someone like Bunyan worth a borrowing after all? As I walked through the wilderness of this world?

Wanting a more Springerishly connotative verb, though. As I wandered? Traipsed? *Shlepped?*

There's Springer, sauntering through the wilderness of this world?

That take him anywhere?

Where it takes him's into no less than twenty-odd pages over the next three days, sing spastic muse!

Semiliterate for the most, scarce a hundred words in the lot he'll probably salvage. Still, roughs out the type-scripted Springer in his spiritual penury and with his spindrift hots, sketches that night with Maggie and some moments with Dana on the morning thereafter. Always happiest drafting rapidly anyhow, rather weigh the architecture first and then so to speak scrimshaw the prose in later. *Chacun à son* spew.

Dane at the office straight through too, unsuspecting of the clacking till she'll wander in on it Saturday. *Salud!* Behold then his quaffed and sullied art!

"Whoever you're writing to there, Lucien, I do hope you'll remember to drop your mother a line also?"

"Listen, hon. It couldn't be sketchier."

"Lucien, don't I know how you work? Let me look."

"Wait, one other thing. I haven't even stopped to think about names yet. Obviously, Springer is essentially me, but I've made up background in which he's screwed someone I actually call Norma Miljus, simply because she was the first regular over there who came to mind. And then I've got him in bed with Maggie too."

"May I see for myself already?"

Modestly necessary preface nonetheless, might one venture? Arrant travestying bastard. Meanwhile what's it taken, weeks of edgy frittering before the actual three days at the machine? So here's professional Dana back in practically the space of a cigarette. Vestige of a smile there, at least?

"Good heavens, what's the theme going to be? Husband's liberation?"

"Hell. Does that mean he comes off as a total chancre?"

"Well now first of all, Lucien, I hope you don't seriously suspect I'm the person to give you an objective reading? But you're probably dead already if it falls into the hands of a woman reviewer. Tell me why the telescoped style, correlative for his state of mind?"

"I suppose. Not much reason to reach for baroque cadences when all he himself is reaching for is the next drink."

"Or the next obliging *derrière*. Where does it go once he does have the affair?"

"I only wish I knew. Meantime I was also wishing someone might suggest it's worth the candle."

"Don't be silly, bits of it had me laughing in spite of myself already. In fact there's only one rather conspicuous flaw."

"Shit. Where?"

"Do you absolutely need that image about my Ruben-esque waistline?"

"Oh, you cluck. Give me a kiss."

Connubial adoration thus yet again reaffirmed, is it? How not, if only after nary a cavil at the sex?

No toilsome *petit-bourgeois* hypocrisy in the Lucien Springer household, by Jesus.

As on she flows, sweet ruptured maidenhead of the mind! Less than a ransacked virgin's notion of what's ahead still, but ah, how beatific's the gush. Eleven solid anchored hours that Sunday, seventeen additional pages foldered. Springer himself quite believe twenty-one on the day following?

Ostensibly fictional Loosh already fictionally fucking the ostensibly fictional Cornford, he'll bray hymeneal hymns of another sort to that *sui generis* arse as well.

Trusting it now too, slovenly as it is. Let the rare lightning strike and Springer's been known to rough out a workable full novel in two weeks, devil take the groanings to come. Just *get it down*, oh terrific, erogenous, hunt in rhapsodies and peck in rigadoons, recollected foreplay of Jessica please nourish him, unforgotten fellatio of Jessica please intoxicate him, *in saecula saeculorum*, break off only once for one near masturbatory remembrance of his unfulfilled upside-down Archimedean dream. Oh lost, and by the lubricants grieved, hillocky hump come back again!

Sursum corda. While's Dana expected to pat his fissured skull over this spate of "creativity" next also?

"Hey, Dane, something that's only now dawning on me. I'm sure I've mentioned how much Jessie's said about herself, and a few fairly stringent confidences are already slipping in. Names alone, for example. You mind not reading any more until I change all that?"

"I'd much rather wait until you're revising anyhow."

Short reprieve, at least. Help if he makes Jess Jewish, maybe? Or just rewrite the Vaseline as bagels and lox?

Speaking of which. How in the rectal heck'd he let it get to be Tuesday afternoon when Jonathan Hundley was leaving on Sunday?

"Hello?"

"Hi. Me. Did you go to Pennsylvania?"

"Oh, hi. No, as a matter of fact. It turned out that he had to rush back after only one day."

Putrescent damn, possible Springer's almost forgotten this sort of jollity for the moment too? Four unaccounted days, is that?

"So what have you been doing?"

"Mostly waiting to hear from my autistic agent. Though I also still never seem to get a minute free, recently."

Rectum? Damned near killed'im. Piss. Dribble. Micturate.

"But tell me about yourself, Lucien?"

"Oh, well, I guess I do have some news. Will you believe seventy pages? Counting the one in the machine?"

"Good grief, you can't be serious? In these few days?"

"Swear on my rusted space bar. As fast as I can type, though, most of it. Just to see how it falls."

"But still. That's spectacular. When may I read some?"

"Let me start a saner draft. Meantime what's on for tonight?"

"Darn it, I've a hunch I'll be stuck late up here. But I will have to eat. Should I look for you?"

"What time?"

"Probably ten, at the earliest."

Just the hour when a Balzac or a Kafka'd be grinding into high gear. So what'd those obsolescent neurotics know?

Quarter to midnight rather, and then it's a call. "Hey, I'm sorry. I wound up having to order in, and then my boss gave me a lift right to the door before I remembered. Do you still feel like coming over?"

"Eight minutes."

Closer to three, Dana be enraptured she's recompensing taxis? And is it jump-suited Jess who's so beautiful, or the figment he's been falling in love with all over again at the typewriter?

"Gosh, have you truly done that many pages?"

"I'm already running out of synonyms for callipygian. Which means immortal of backside. And do me a favor by thinking of a name for yourself, will you?"

"But for now you're writing everything the way it happened? And using people I've told you about?"

"How not? All those phantoms you fuck."

"Listen, I did say I don't mind. But you will eventually disguise everyone?"

"Jess, now hell. If you want I'll even let you go through the whole mess later on with a red pencil. Only your dirty menstrual underdrawers have to stay sacrosanct." Sharing wine, they'll camp amid the pillows. "So meantime, just to keep this rote version straight. Who were you screwing that you wouldn't tell me about a couple of weeks ago?"

"Lucien, Lucien, we've done this. Be Conradian. Suffuse your prose with ambiguity."

"Suffuse your twat, twat."

Amused where she'll imbibe. Andrea Mantegna was Giovanni Bellini's brother-in-law, Springer plan to let Springer beggar himself like this in the manuscript also? That fawning jock fishmonger after all, Rosen? Why else the sudden slobbery good-bye if they hadn't been bedded?

"Lucien, stop acting so morose. What I said about pro-
tecting people is all the more relevant now. I certainly don't
want anyone to be hurt."

"Don't think you won't get yours, though. In fact I
just may decide to call you Susanna. Swipe all the rest of
the names from your own book too."

"Oh, glory, wouldn't that be sort of a gas? For all the
zillions who'll read us both."

Girl's delighted, Springer'll ruffle hair and press her
down. Then playful and oniony's their kiss. She seeming
wan there, however?

"I really couldn't be more pleased that you're working.
It's even kind of gutsy, do you know?"

"What are you talking about?"

"No, I mean it. After how long you've been out of
things."

"You're my new muse."

"Bullshit."

"Fact." Springer'll chew at her chin. "Though a pretty
raggedy one. Are you half as beat as you suddenly look?"

"I guess I am, sort of. Besides the long day, I was up
until all hours last night."

Again, again, again. Who? What?

"You want to get to sleep?"

"I guess I ought to, truthfully."

Kick himself for the offering, generous gelded Jesus.

"Forgive me, Lucien. I should have realized before I
called."

Drink while she'll climb and stretch, whole chapel by
Mantegna bombed to smithereens in World War II? Then
lean at the bedroom door with Jessie nakeding beyond,
nightgown shimmied into from under. So matter of fact
and for granted taken. Yet when'd they make love last,
where's this seeping away to?

[208]

"And it's all my own gleepy fault. That new book on Trotsky out front, I started about half-past twelve. Thinking I'd browse a little. So the next thing I knew it was twenty minutes to five."

"Oh, damn, there are times when I do cherish you. One kiss between the yawns, at least."

Hold her the moment, hands beneath eftsoons. And ah, alack, no figment's this.

"Ummm, stop. You'll leave me all goosebumpy."

"Tush, tush, thy *tush*."

Slithering away. "Good night, drippy."

"Good night, *shtunk*."

And so. And so. End his book with right now, at least solder in its subtle, unsuspected political *motif*? Springer mulcted out of a fuck by a pickaxed Bolshevik?

Or's a queer semiperhaps insight almosting as he'll away? Jessie's tears, he recalling? One chance in ten thousand, possible it's he himself she's pined for, or did the once? Pages he'll just next be trying in fact, Springer turning tail after their first few unbelievable nights, Jess maybe more wounded than he selfishly ever perceived or found guts to inquire?

"Oh, fool, sapient fool, can you suspect I ever wanted any of those others, my very groin's soul benumbed by strangers? All were bulwarks against you, you, oh wretched varlet Lucien Springer, whom I knew I might never wholly possess!"

Then watch in stoical bereavement as she dashes sobbing to where the convent gates envelop her?

Remarkable syndrome for all that. Cataleptic for practically a year, bang away like a madman once he's finally at it. Dozen hours daily's the least now.

Dubious moments too, however. He going to admit to all that defaulted sex? Ever been a novel in which the only graphic climaxes are the ones the hero doesn't give the heroine?

Brood upon something else as well, *viz.* that question of just how much she ever maybe wanted him after all. Nub of the book's Springer's own omphalos-gazing, true, but's Jess ever said one word about what she really feels?

Again, Springer ever asked? Rip at him whichever way she bent.

So meanwhile how's he also let another four or five days pass? This a Sunday? Dana and the kids both, grab a pay phone under pretext of cigarettes.

"Lucien, *comment allez-vous?* Are you still you should pardon me upchucking onward?"

"Plow deep while sluggards sleep. How's close to another hundred pages sound?"

"Now stop. It isn't possible."

"You working yourself?"

"Really no. Someone's been staying with me."

That the phone gurgling or his abdomen? Euchred shit.

"It's my old roommate. From San Francisco, I think I mentioned her husband being here once. In fact, listen, we were just rushing out."

"Go, go."

Incredible, thirty seconds including the aborted internal tumult and still, all maladies into remission. Make a *novena* if her chum'd stay through the draft.

Minute after he's back be typing his merry ass off again.

"*Nu?* So how's it scan?"

"Jessie's convinced I must regurgitate the stuff. At this rate I'll have to call her for a date next week to find out what happens next."

"Pretty funny. Do I start clocking the obituaries again?"

"I'll probably be using that very business in a day or two. I'm being as kind to you as I'm able, incidentally."

"You didn't say I figure in it, Loosh? Listen, bardic ego's at stake, how am I yclept?"

"You tell me. I'm letting the first version run verbatim."

"What? You're not perverse enough to have Cornford in there by name too?"

"Oh, well, I told you Dana knows we're thick."

"*Oy, Gevalt.*" Pike'll set soda aside sighing. "All right, Lucien. It's your marriage."

"Hi, sweetheart. Working?"

"Is it possible to contract herpes zoster of the spine?"

"Whatever it is I'm all for it. Listen, will you mind if dinner is late? There's a cocktail party I forgot. For some political magazine people."

Springer's amused, Jess maybe included? "Whenever's fine."

Set him to ruminating, however. Book's crying out for an encounter, knows. Love to fabricate one, or'll reality hold him constrained?

Imagine Jess there tonight in fact, Dane spotting her from the photo? Same first glance and damned well comprehend he'd crawl to Hyderabad and back to poke his nose into that slit?

Or send them glissading off for a private drink together, why not? Forty minutes of Dana's Vermeer composure and Jess repudiate all future homewrecking for sisterhood and solidarity?

Stunning, worst comes to worst Springer'll bind off his whelpy first draft that way. Hero's alone scratching his sprockets while the pair of them talk Doris Lessing until three A.M.

So who next meanwhile?

"Lucien, hello. I just got word from my agent."

"Hey. And?"

"I can't believe it. He seems to like it almost as much as you do."

"Did I tell you? Where's he submitting to?"

"Well, he thinks it might be smart if I do a précis of the rest first."

"So when do you give notice?"

"Let me see how snotty the first rejection letters are. But what about you?"

"Next sheet I put in will be number one-nine-five."

"Good Lord. I'm jealous, I swear."

"Jess, as someone said, there's a difference between writing and typewriting. Your girlfriend pack up?"

"Yesterday, yes."

Full week already since their memorial non-boff for the proletarian revolution? "What's on tonight?"

"I should really start outlining that synopsis. And there's a party I may or may not stop at first. Do you want to try me around eleven?"

Life about to anticipate art after all, tra-la?

Manipulate both of them back here together, even? Hmmm. Jess all averted countenance and shyly pawing, say? While Dane's abrim with nobility, hand upon her heart? Oh, deedy. "Lucien, dear Jessica's told me everything. Everything. I understand, and I cannot remain in your way. I'll send enough money to support the two of you in Mexico, burden though it will be. All I ask is that you write often to the children."

Embracing and weeping anon each. Jessie's flung herself to the rug, she'll clasp Dana's hem.

"Hence, hence. Go, thee, and be fruitful in one another."

Fade to Elysium. See Loosh giggle. See Loosh shut the typewriter and revive his empty glass.

He intend to include this sort of idiocy when he gets this far along also?

Right after the sections about world ecological imbalance and irreversible population increase and the plight of Israel.

Never the twain. Unless simultaneously a cozy weewee in adjacent stalls unbeknownst, mayhap?

"So. What's your status?"

"I haven't gotten that much done. But I was just broiling a hamburger, why not come while I take the break?"

Peepee of his own first, gift of any new graffiti to enthrall his beloved?

I'd rather fuck the pizza and eat the waitress.

Lipp Pike did. He says the pizza's better.

Meantime what's taking a break mean exactly, codpiece again tonight? Screw the synecdoche likewise.

"Garlic, garlic, garlic."

"Tough, tough, tough. Which reminds me. I think I'm sore at you."

"Can't occur. About what?"

"For a while I couldn't figure it out. Why am I annoyed with Lucien? You keep announcing all those page numbers."

"Hell, I told you. Nine tenths of it is run Spot run."

"Oh, probably I mean all that freedom. Having a husband like Dana to support you."

"Trull. I hope you realize it's a pretty meager chunk out of eighteen years. Fair's fair."

Sorting herself amid the pillows, why's he not following? Gauzy blouse also, infer the touch of her from here. Now 'swounds, pigeon-liver'd he feeling?

"So what else is up?"

"I'm bedraggled. My girlfriend cost me forever, Phoebe Cissell has troubles she seems to think I can't live without, and now Adam Herschberger is after me for a few days in the Hamptons."

Modigliani died in a pauper's ward. "Can I assume that last one sort of comes from left field?"

"Oh, I could handle it. And he also has children who'd be there. But anyway, I told him I simply have to get back to work."

Lolling now, all indolence. And still mongrel Loosh'll secretly cower. On his mind too often's the crux, positive he'd muck it anew. Time, time, ah damn, Dana weekending somewhere ever?

Or's this emulsifying as their pattern finally, Springer evolve into one of the prattling eunuchs altogether? Like Max? Gourmet dinners as a threesome next, do try the truffles? Oh, help, can't stand it.

Can't cope with it either, not tonight, let it baste until the book's on paper at least. "Well, fie."

"Fie?"

"Your synopsis. Before I become an appendix to that shit list myself."

Vagueness when she'll rise, however, no sign either way. What thinking, what? Eternally, ever know?

"Golly, though. You'll have it finished in no time?"

"To where it rolls over limp in the middle of a solipsism."

"Maybe I'll call Dana."

"And?"

"Howdy, there. We haven't met, but my name is Jessica Cornford. I've been thinking we ought to give Lucien a party."

Fist along her cheek. "Better wait until the next draft. By which time I'll have been thrown out of the house."

"Lucien, what she knows she knows already."

"Jess, I've got everything in there from the taste of your urethra to the acoustics in your womb."

"Oh, Lordy. Sometimes I'm not sure I'll want to read it myself."

"Fucking well will. If only to see how much I've suf-
fered."

"Dork."

Dana manage a little sympathy too, come to think on
it? Find out a married man's passion's hardly all titties and
skittles?

"Anyway, anyway."

At the door, so here's that sometime Gauguin look in
the oblique light to rend him now also, almost unconscion-
able's such loveliness. Hands at her shoulders, dear Hermes
the ache.

"I'll call you."

"Work nice."

Y basta? Springer truly stroll out that idly?

So now's he sensing she'd have been receptive even?
What in her mind if she was? Suspect he's easing out of
it himself maybe, breaking it off?

Cockatrice paradoxes'll throttle him, now *merde*. Run
back, grab her in his arms? "Jess, Jess, who gives a tinker's
barf about books, writing, anything? Let's just fuck! Let's
fuck!"

"Lucien, the pizza's better."

Saloon again rather hastily instead?

Saloon.

Springer at least cognizant of the signal themes in that giglot manuscript of his, is he?

Indubitably. *Uno*: he ever going to make Jess come again? *Dos*: how's she really feel about all this bilge?

Anything else perhaps subordinate and/or ancillary yet permeative?

Indubitably. Whatever happened to that south slope and the Sherpa porters?

Any titles pending which allude to or insinuate the foregoing, preferably in corresponding sequence if so?

Indubitably. *The Once and Future Orgasm. Cornfroy's Complaint. Sometimes a Great Keester.*

Listen, blotterbrain, try to be sober for seventeen seconds. Your problematical ending beside the point, what do you ultimately want out of this coprophagous excursus?

Oh, words, obviously.

Meaning?

Play a little. With luck a phrase or three worth some lonely pretty girl's midnight underlining.

What've phrases got to do with the cost of smoked salmon in Abu Dhabi?

Haven't I acknowledged that? Just once, can't a character be the product of his own fucked-up head rather than society?

That account for all the pretentious literary *disjecta membra* in there too?

Don't call me pretentious to vindicate your own long-rationalized surrenders, mate. What should occupy him instead, how many citizens of Warsaw does it take to change a light bulb? In any case he himself won't be writing for people who can only read long books because they haven't the time to read short ones.

Neat line, except you even borrowed that. Pascal? Meanwhile what about readers who'll splutter over vocabulary alone?

Again, what are you accusing me of except the corrosion in your own tool chest?

Now tell me that a book is a mirror and if a jackass looks in a wit can scarcely be expected to look out. Schopenhauer this time? I believe you'd better take a gander at this.

Qué es eso?

You copied it out whimsically yourself. A few years ago. I am not by nature a person much moved by pure language? Now what in the carnal Gehenna's that supposed to mean? That Samuel Beckett better watch his ass? That James Joyce better? Can the man even know what it is he *thinks* he's admitting? Who'd say a thing like that?

Christopher Lehmann-Haupt. Have fun, author.

"Are you honestly only two or three days from finishing?"

"Only if you've got a spare *deus ex machina* lying around? Should I put this out?"

"Thank you. Have him abruptly eaten by a vexed unicorn?"

"I'd been leaning toward a monsoon. Listen, I suspect you're going to abominate the bloody thing, by the way."

"Sweetheart? Why would I?"

"Oh, Springer and his leaky hots. It's every page."

"Isn't that what the book was supposed to be from the start?"

"Still. Anyway."

"What, Lucien?"

"I guess I might as well say. I have been sort of hung up on her, Dane."

Immaculate, the silence. And where in the name of gulled incredulous Joseph'd that come from?

"Oh, well, after all. A girl that attractive, seeing her fairly often."

So now remote. "And?"

"And what? The predictable untidy menopausal letch, is all. I hope you're not about to take it the wrong way?"

"Precisely what would you suggest is the right way?"

"Dane, now hell. Look how washed out and costive I was, it's actually even been damned salutary for me. I do owe it to her that I'm finally back into something. Oh, probably I owe Maggie too, in a rather different sense. But it even shows in the manuscript. The very prose doesn't quite plug in until Springer himself's gotten *connected* again."

"How nice for the very prose."

"Stop. You know the finished book will be dedicated to you."

"While just imagine, all those other benighted wives who settle for kitchen help. Or a summer home. I've just thought of an ending for you."

"You're sure you don't want to take a minute to revise?"

"And lived happily ever after. Up to their elbows in scarcely much more *dreck* than usual. Lucien, Lucien. Will you at least get rid of that cigarette and make love to me, please?"

So. Precisely what and to what extent of same does Springer believe he's let rear its opprobrious head?

Gratuitous verification of heretofore uncensured and very possibly unsuspicioned infatuation and/or desire. Though as it were a mere and reasonably explicable eighteen-year itch. Fescennine fatuity.

Did he or did he not imply fulfillment thereof, however?

Proposition's suffused with ambiguity. Though neither obviously did Dana further inquire.

Conclusions appertaining *re* this latter curiosity?

Rather not know herself, presumably.

Springer beset by any fulsome compulsions to resume said confessional on his own part, then?

Once, a philosopher. Twice, a pervert.

It was I killed the old pawnbroker woman and her sister with an axe and robbed them?

So we beat on, boats against the current, borne back ceaselessly into the past?

Reader, I married him?

All at once she thought of the man crushed by the train the day she had first met Vronsky, and she knew what she had to do?

It is a far, far better thing that I do than I have ever done?

Isn't it pretty to think so?

And the great shroud of the sea rolled on as it rolled five thousand years ago?

Thus they held funeral for Hector, tamer of horses?

Somebody threw a dead dog after him down the ravine?

Whoever you are, I have always depended on the kindness of strangers?

Ugly hell, gape not? Come not, Lucifer?

What a pretty girl, what nice legs?

Between grief and nothing I will take grief?

Poo-tee-weet?

Ah, Bartleby? Ah, humanity?

More light?

She was a real blonde?

So I awoke, and behold it was a dream?

I have caused thee to see it with thine eyes, but thou shalt not go over thither?

Ite, missa est?

Our revels now are ended?

Good night, sweet prince?

Zymosis, zymotic, zymurgy, zyzzyva?

One to hold the bulb and three to rotate the table?

"Lipp, mockery may well be the only word for it. About four hours at the desk tomorrow and I'll be caught up to this very phone call. And then what? Can anybody in history ever have written anything this way?"

"Anne Frank. But for Christ's sake, give somebody besides me credit for the line."

Dramatically shred the whole *megillah* sheet by sheet, maybe?

"Jesus, and he'd said it was going well. But even if Dana could have glued the stuff back together, there was all that blood on it."

Or having admitted the generalization, perhaps ironically salvage the book by now averring the particulars also? "Dane, every scurvy comma's true. And for my last chapter, would you mind terribly if I bring in the tape recorder once you've finished reading?"

Let the street be as wide as the height of the houses. Unquote, Leonardo. And incidentally how many days since he's called Jess this time? Magnify that suggestion he's retreating? Shambling woebegone shit.

"You want to hit me with another one of these, Mike?"

"And Mike, is his credit good for a Campari and soda too?"

Strive to imitate Michelangelo in all things. Vasari. Dear Lord, so in tonight's light those cheekbones alone.

"Sneaky, you are."

"I was having dinner with a friend. And then I realized something dreadful."

Uther Pendragon is dead. Also she has to cash a check.

"Probably there's something waiting in the mail from my family. Another hour and a half and it will be my birthday."

"Hey. You never did say exactly when."

"Can I really be twenty-six?"

"Old and gray and abusing herself by the fire."

"Stop, it's grim enough. In fact my last girlish moments, can we sort of gulp these and maybe walk somewhere for a while?"

Gulped. Walking. Bedfordward? Sprucien Loosh and Cessican Jess, and which one took which's hand?

"Oh, impossible scut Jessica Louise."

"Says how?"

"I couldn't have been more depressed in there. So here's she and already mostly healed's he."

"What were you depressed about?"

"You've got me interdicted against telling you. But by tomorrow afternoon Springer'll have to disappear into an open manhole."

"Glory, but that means it *exists*, just about. Something will surely come when you start sifting back through it?"

"Oh, it's more than that anyhow."

Eye him questioning as they stroll.

"All damned day, limning someone named Cornford. And Springer, by the way. Our Eleusinian names, I'd never noticed. But I suspect I half hoped the process might turn cathartic, get you out of my system that way."

Consider him silently still.

"So instead I sit there with my insides churning."

Springer imagining things, or'd this self-counseling creature squeeze his hand? Jessie, Jessie, Jessie, just once will you ever maybe when the subject's us *say something*?

"Anyway, screw all my own halfassed leaden-eyed dross. Do have a good year, will you?"

"Thank you."

"And listen. Because I mean this. For all my sleaziness in trying to have things both ways, Jess. It would tear me up if you found somebody. But I do want you to be happy."

"I know you do, Lucien."

Springer'll grin, enoughing that. "Whatever the deuce your other name is going to be. How about one of those Dickensian exaggerations, best of your personality in a word? Miss Fanny Bottomley, say?"

"Moke."

"I think in revision I'll give you chronic postnasal clap. Or an obscure tattoo just inside your thigh, and whenever Springer asks you'll shudder mysteriously. But let me tell you my one real blunder, distress critics for centuries. I've come up with these great lines for Springer when he falls to brooding, all about an undiscovered country from whose bourn no traveler returns. Except it slipped my mind I'd already shown him with his father's ghost."

All smile's Jess, did squeeze now for a fact. "Spring, Spring. That's odd, nobody ever seems to call you that. Let me tell you something instead."

"Tell."

"But don't take it the wrong way, will you? Since I'm not even sure how I mean it. Maybe feeling sentimental because of what day it almost is. And I did hope you'd be there when I stopped by."

"Jess?"

"I do sort of love you, if somehow you haven't known?"

"Oh, Lucien! Oh, Lucien! Oh, Lucien! Oh, Lucien! Oh, Lucien! Oh, Lucien! Oh, Lucien!"

"Oh, Jesus. Oh, seismographic Christ!"

"God. God. Where did that come from?"

"Don't question genius. Oh, help. Oh, help."

"Lucien, dear Lord. Was it *nine*? Multiple is multiple, but could I possibly have come *nine consecutive times*? I may never play my bull fiddle again. Let alone walk."

"Happy birthday."

"Thank you. Oh, wow, and do I mean thank you."

Nine? For Springer's once?

NINE?

And then laughter. Half demented still from their miracle he's suddenly awash in it, Springer's clutching immemorial Jess and he's commenced to shake and shake.

"Lucien, what?"

Can't stop, he's inveigled so. While all froth and foam and gunk and goo they are too, how'd Jessie even get jism on the tip of her nose?

"Now good grief?"

"Oh, nuncle. My book. How it ends. The very last sentence, even."

"Well, tell me."

"I can't, it's so ridiculous. And I love it. Oh, no."

"Lucien, for mercy's sake?"

"What else? What else? To be continued!"

"Lucien, you categorically cannot end a novel by saying to be continued."

"Wouldn't it sure as hell seem the present disposition of my materials?"

"Oh, glory."

Springer's finally disengaged, he'll fetch smokes. While there's Jess mirthful and sated, life's insane.

"Lucien, I repeat. You simply can't."

"As a matter of fact I almost do begin to wonder why not. Do you really believe anything ever changes, Jess? Tell me about that bright morning when you're even going to straighten up this mangy apartment. Or watch me myself sweat a year revising this one new short book and then gurgle back into another boozy, indeterminate malaise. Because of reviewers with no ear, or whatever other excuse. Meanwhile what more than locking in some few bittersweet moments, if I can, my ha'penny love story, ask the *nihil obstat* for that and laughter alone?"

"What does *nihil obstat* mean?"

"Nothing stands in the way. The Catholic censor uses it. Nothing obstructs."

"Oh, I guess maybe it is comic, sort of. Or at least so you can finish your first draft."

Touch of wistfulness there too, somehow? Springer's sitting, he'll press knuckles to Jessie's wetted breast.

"Anyhow, I want to tell you something. Something else that won't change."

"What, Lucien?"

"I love Dana. Out of more than just old habit or the decades shared. I *love* her."

"Haven't I known you do?"

"I also love you. And out of more than just my beleaguered ardor for your rapidly aging pussy. Even if I do understand how you meant it when you said that yourself, Jess."

"I'm glad. Golly, didn't the one sentence work wonders, though?"

"So in a week or two my kids will scoot off to camp, and then Dana will do a couple of visits somewhere. Naturally just when Jonathan Hundley decides to appear. Or some stout young conquistador you won't even identify."

"Lucien, don't plan."

"Come shower with me."

"I think tonight I ought to soap your hair again."

"Oh, damn. Oh, old horse Jess."

Clasp her anew, they'll cleave still liquidy there awhile, serene. Springer with his book in his arms.

Or until Jessie's the one laughing now. Quietly aquiver she'll become.

"Tell me."

"Oh, Lordy. What time is it?"

"Actually it's early. Why?"

"How incredible I feel. Would that be what made me remember? I think I did something shameless."

"Jessie?"

"Weeks and weeks and weeks ago. Are you certain it's early?"

"Jess, will you say it, already?"

"Oh, dear. Right behind you, then. In that bottom drawer."

"Darn this, now. What is?"

"Well what would you guess? Or can it be so long that you've forgotten all about it? Dopey. The Vaseline."

Once, a philosopher?

"Oh, Lucien. Oh, my God!"
"Is this what that thing's about in *Romeo and Juliet*? Not so deep as a well, nor so wide as a church door?"
"Oh, Lucien. Oh, oh, oh, oh!"
"Or in *Ecclesiastes*? God made man upright, but they have sought out many inventions? Listen, which is steeper, Annapurna or Kanchenjunga?"
"Oww, I think I need my mother again. *Oh!*"
"Holy smokes. Wait, now. Don't move. Wait."
"Lucien? Oh, dear heaven. *Oh, good grief!*"
"Sweet grommeted eureka. Jess? Very gingerly. Turn your head so we can look at each other."
"Lucien? How?"
"Maybe with a wild surmise? Silent, upon a peak in Darien?"

Nihil obstat.

"But, hey. Did you ever read Malory? *Le Morte D'Arthur?*"

"God above, is there anyone else alive who would ask a question like that at a moment like this?"

"That famous line about Guinevere, is all. While she lived she was a true lover. And therefore she had a good end."

"Oh, glory. Are you sure it isn't time for you to have to hurry home after all?"

"Just keep holding still. I forgot Winston Churchill."

"Imbecile. My finest hour again?"

"Better. For my book, too. This is not the end. It is not even the beginning of the end. But it is, perhaps, the end of the beginning."

"Lucien, Lucien, Lucien."

"Jess, Jess, Jess."

"Lucien? *Oh, Lucien! Oh, oh, oh, Lucien, oh!*"

Being continued.